31 July 2020

Priscilla
the
Princess
of the
Park

Mandy— Thank you for your wisdom and kindness w/Maggie!

Pat LaMarche
Bonnie Tweedy Shaw

She loved your school!

Pat la Marche

For Ronan

who wisely counseled me to
explain homelessness using
a chapter book for kids

Table of Contents

CHAPTER 1

Magdalena

Magdalena put her hands up by her ears, grabbed her hair and flipped it behind her. Nothing irritated Magdalena more than when her hair fell down in front of her shoulders. She wanted to cut it. Her dad wouldn't hear of it. He always said, "Magdalena, you have such beautiful hair. Your curls remind me of my grandmother, and she never cut her hair. Not once in all the time I knew her."

Magdalena believed the stories her dad told about great grandma Harriet. She sounded wonderful. But seriously, what kid wanted to have a hairstyle from the 1960s? Every time Magdalena's dad told her why he liked her hair, Magdalena wanted to cut it even more.

Maggie, she preferred Maggie, reached into her pocket and pulled out a scrunchy. She pulled her thick black curls to the back of her head and made a ponytail. With her mass of hair finally under control, Maggie put her arms through her backpack straps and started to run. Only four blocks from home, Maggie couldn't wait to get to her room and hide her new-found treasure.

"Hey, hey, not so fast." Her mom reached over and scooped Maggie up as she ran through the front door. "I'm pretty sure nobody gets into this house without paying the toll." Maggie harrumphed, rolled her eyes and pursed her lips to kiss her mom squarely on the cheek.

"That's better." Shewan, Maggie's mom, let her slip out of her arms – inch by inch – until her feet touched the ground. "Why's my Miss Magdalena in such a hurry today?" She asked.

There was that name again.

Maggie replied, "You know none of my friends can spell my name."

Shewan stared down her nose at her daughter and said, "Well, of course they can't. They're only eight. But when you're all fifteen you'll have the coolest name in the crowd."

Unconvinced, Maggie headed for the stairs.

"Hey, you didn't answer me," her mom called up the stairs after her. But that child was gone.

The hallway at the top of the stairs had three closed doors. The one on the right went to the bathroom. Maggie zipped past it. She bolted past one on the left too. That door led to her parents' room. The paint in the hallways was the same color as the trim work and the doors. It would have looked quite drab if not for Maggie's room – the one at the end of the hall. Maggie stopped running just shy of smashing into her door. She pulled her backpack off and fumbled in the front pocket. Her hand fished around feeling for the purple satin ribbon her dad had fastened to the skeleton key that unlocked the big brass lock. Gabriel, Maggie's dad, installed the device after about three months of begging. "Okay, Maggie." Her dad obliged her request to shorten her name if not her hair. "I'll give you a lock for your door. But your mom and I are keeping a copy of the key. We'll never invade your privacy, but we want you to be responsible and let us in when we knock."

Those rules seemed fair enough to Maggie. She trusted her parents. She just wanted privacy. Besides, if they had a key, she'd never get locked out if she lost the one she carried on the ribbon.

About the time Maggie got to her room, Shewan appeared on the landing behind her. "What's so exciting that you had to run right past your very own mother who waits all day to see you?" Her mom had gotten more curious with every step up the stairs.

Maggie pushed her door inward. Suddenly the entire second floor brightened. Nothing about Maggie's room looked anything like the dull hallway that led to it. The late afternoon sun still shone brightly through the sheer purple curtains hanging from golden rods. Her four-poster bed had purple curtains as well. The comforter on her bed was bright pink with purple starbursts all over it. Books and a few dolls littered the deep lime green carpet on the floor.

"Now don't tell me you ran up here to clean your room before dinner." Her mom teased playfully. "I'll have to call Doctor LeBlanc and have you checked."

"Mom," Maggie rolled her eyes. Maggie seldom called

Shewan mom. She'd stopped about a year earlier. Long about the tenth or eleventh time Shewan forgot to call Magdalena Maggie, Maggie decided to call her mom anything she wanted to too.

Funny thing was, Shewan liked it. Shewan thought it showed an independent streak in her daughter. In Shewan's mind, independence was one of the most important character traits a girl could have. Cultivating that independence was the reason Shewan talked Gabriel into putting the lock on Magdalena's door.

She insisted even.

"Look Gabriel, Magdalena needs her own space. A big old-fashioned golden lock and key fits perfectly with that fancy room of hers. She won't lock us out too long. But she'll know we trust her and that will boost her confidence," Shewan explained.

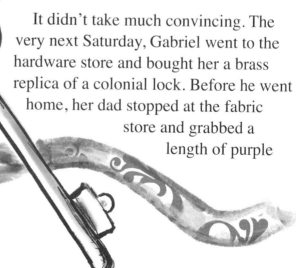

It didn't take much convincing. The very next Saturday, Gabriel went to the hardware store and bought her a brass replica of a colonial lock. Before he went home, her dad stopped at the fabric store and grabbed a length of purple

4

ribbon too. When Gabriel showed it to Shewan she smiled. "That kid'll be thrilled," she said.

Now, with her hand still on the doorknob Maggie looked back over her shoulder and sighed. "Oh all right. Come in here and I'll show you what Priscilla gave me today."

At the mention of Priscilla's name, Shewan's hands went to her hips and her eyes looked up at the ceiling. "Ahh, you saw Priscilla today, did you?"

Maggie knew her mom didn't believe that Priscilla was real. At first it irritated her that her mom thought she had an imagined an entire woman and everything about her. But after a while it didn't matter at all.

As a precaution, Shewan had hired a babysitter to stay at the park with Maggie every time she went, so she knew Magdalena was safe while visiting her "imaginary friend." Of course, Shewan could just ask Lani about Priscilla – but she wouldn't. Since Shewan was so convinced that Magdalena had invented the woman, she opted not to mention Priscilla to anyone. Shewan wouldn't embarrass her daughter by letting a sixteen-year-old sitter know that Maggie had imaginary friends.

Still standing in the doorway, Maggie could have kicked herself. She'd broken her own rule. Maggie promised herself that she wouldn't mention Priscilla at home unless she had no choice. Maggie didn't like telling her mom about her visits with Priscilla. Not because they weren't exciting – Maggie didn't like to tell Shewan because they ended up having such a one-sided conversation.

Today was no different.

"Who is Priscilla again?" Shewan tried to trip her little girl up. Shewan frequently asked the same question to see if Maggie would answer the same way she always did.

Maggie didn't care. Maggie smiled. Maggie beamed, in fact. Maggie loved Priscilla, and she was happy to retell her mom who Priscilla was. "Oh Shewan, you know who Priscilla is. Priscilla is the Princess of the Park."

CHAPTER 2

Tomas

Hugo walked up the tree-lined street towing Tomas by the wrist. Tomas pulled at each of Hugo's fingers trying to loosen his big brother's grip. Hugo's large hand wrapped the whole way around Tomas' lower arm – and then some. Even when Tomas succeeded in prying one of Hugo's fingers open, the other four held tight.

"You know Mama yells at me when you don't come straight home, Tomas. Then she makes me come looking for you and drag you home. Aren't you getting sick of this yet?" Hugo asked but kept walking. Four years older and a whole foot taller, Hugo walked even faster than Tomas could run.

Tomas yelled, "Hugo, slow down. I'm running and I can't keep up with you. You're going to rip my arm out of its socket."

Hugo ignored him and charged on toward the brown brick apartment complex where Hugo, Tomas and their sister Sofia all lived with their parents and their Bela. "Lucky for you Mama and Papa aren't home. Bela sent me looking for you. She won't tell on us but one of these days she won't be there. You have to come straight home from school, Tomas."

Suddenly Hugo stopped. He yanked on Tomas and bent down to look in his face. "Tell me Tomas, why do you spend all afternoon at the park with that old woman?"

Tomas stared blankly at his big brother. Hugo watched Tomas' eyes fill with tears. Still, braver than usual in the face of his brother's taunts, Tomas kept staring. Then with sudden force, Tomas jerked his hand back and pulled free. The whole escape shocked Hugo. Hugo thought about acting mad but decided against it. He chuckled instead, "I let you go. We are almost home now. I wouldn't want Bela to see me manhandling you anyway. You are her pet, you know."

Tomas smiled his first smile of their high-speed walk home. "I know," he replied.

Hugo lunged forward, chest out like he would body slam

his younger sibling. But they both knew he was only kidding. They giggled. They knew if Bela looked out the window she would see that they were both safe and quit worrying. They didn't need to hurry any longer. The boys dawdled and chased after each other. Hugo wanted a little time to finish their conversation. Hugo asked his question another way, "Why do you like her so much?"

Tomas smiled and answered, "She's smart. She teaches me things. She knows so much about the flowers and the animals that live in the park."

Hugo ran his hand up over his face and laced his fingers into the front of his hair. He couldn't believe his ears. "You talk to that lady in the park for hours because she knows about daisies and squirrels?"

Tomas cackled. He couldn't believe his brother knew so little about the park. He filled his chest full of air and huffed it back at his brother, "Ha! There are a lot more than squirrels and daisies there!" Now Tomas almost sounded like the encyclopedia at school, "There are many genera of animals and plants thriving in that urban greenery. Squirrels are just one genus."

"Genus? What does that mean? You mean genius?" Hugo asked, legitimately confused.

"No, I mean genus. G-E-N-U-S. I can sure tell you're no genius. You don't even know what a genus is," Tomas snapped.

Hugo looked hurt. Tomas instantly felt bad. His big brute of a brother loved him enough to come looking for him every day and never ratted him out to his parents. Anyway, Tomas knew that Hugo already took a lot of guff at school for not being as smart as his little brother.

Besides, Priscilla never made fun of Tomas a few months back when he didn't know what genus meant. And of all the people alive in the world, Tomas most wanted to be like Priscilla. Tomas looked down, "I'm sorry, Hugo. That wasn't very nice. I shouldn't be mean. Priscilla would be disappointed in me if she knew I made fun of you."

Hugo still looked sad, but he ran his hand up over his face and forehead again and said, "Aw, never mind. I'm never going to be the smart kid in this family. That's your job – if you live long enough to do it. But mom and dad are going to kill you if you don't start getting home before the streetlights come on. Although, I might go to bat for you visiting with Priscilla if she teaches you to quit picking on me about my lousy brains."

They were approaching the wide brick steps that lead to the front doorway of their apartment complex. When Tomas heard what Hugo said about sticking up for him visiting Priscilla in the park, he whipped around so fast he almost slammed straight into one of their neighbors. Mr. Tanis had stepped outside with his miniature poodle, Bertha, for a walk. "Oh, hey, sorry Mr. Tanis, didn't see you there," Tomas blurted. Then in the same breath he addressed his brother, "Would you really Hugo? Would you talk to Mama, Papa and Bela? Would you tell them it's okay that I sit with her after school?"

"Nah," said Hugo. "I'm not going to tell them anything of

the kind. They won't want you talking to some old lady in the park. Best we never mention her at all. You know though, you might persuade me to hang out with you one or two days a week if you'll help me with my math homework."

Hugo's younger brother's eyes narrowed as he sneered up at him, "You mean if I do your math homework!"

Hugo clapped his hands together and copped an arrogant attitude like he'd just cured cancer, "Hey, that sounds like a good idea to me."

Tomas rocked his head back and forth, "It'll never work. Priscilla won't hang out with me if she thinks I'm cheating for you. She'd be really disappointed. Priscilla 'don't tolerate no dishonesty.' She tells us that all the time."

Tomas looked concerned, then his face brightened, "But I could help you for real with your homework!" He exclaimed. "You stay with me Tuesdays and Thursdays in the park after school and Mondays and Wednesdays I'll help you with that pre-algebra that's kicking your butt."

They shook hands as a rather impatient neighbor pulled the door open and asked, "You two coming inside or what?" The brothers ran into the lobby racing for the elevator buttons to see who would push the *UP* button first.

CHAPTER 3

Jillian

Jillian rolled over to let Toby lick the other side of her face. No cat ever loved a little girl more and no little girl ever got out of bed with a better scrubbed face.

Jillian's mom Vivian pushed her wheelchair away from the bed and sat down. "Is Toby done with your cat bath, madam? I wouldn't want to interrupt your grooming with a real washcloth or a reminder to brush your teeth. Or has Toby done that for you too?"

"Blech, Mom," Jillian wrinkled up her nose, "I do draw the line somewhere you know."

Jillian's mom continued, "Well, I woke up late which means you woke up late. The county bus will be here to get you in about eight minutes."

"Good grief, Mom," Jillian hollered, "I can't get ready in eight minutes."

"You can if I help you," her mom pulled back the covers and gently lifted her daughter out of bed. "I'll carry you to the bathroom and help you with your pants. Luckily you laid your clothes out last night. Then I'll put you in your chair and you can wheel yourself down to the end of the walk and wait for Mr. Hutchins to come by with the van."

Vivian began combing her daughter's hair with what looked like a plastic fish. Jillian liked the comb because it had wide gaps between the teeth and detangled her fine blonde hair without hurting her scalp.

"I thought I'd give you $2.20 for breakfast at school, but Mrs. Parker tells me you don't get breakfast on the mornings when you're rushed. She told me that you use the money at the school store to buy granola bars."

Vivian's voice sounded sweet but bewildered. She paused and looked into her daughter's face. "I guess there's nothing wrong with eating granola bars, but why not eat the breakfast? If you like granola bars so much better, I could just buy a box of them at the store, you know."

Jillian snapped to attention in her chair, startling her mom, "Oh, you could? Yes Mom, please. Please buy granola bars."

Vivian regained her composure and pretended not to hear the excited interruption, "Mrs. Parker tells me she's never actually seen you eat the granola bars either, though. She said sometimes you get crackers from her office in the morning. So do you like the granola bars or don't you? Why are you buying them and then eating crackers when your tummy growls?"

Jillian had wheeled over to the sink her dad installed in the bathroom when she was only two years old. It was lower than

14

the regular vanity and had room underneath so she could pull all the way up in her wheelchair. With the help of the lower sink, Jillian could brush her teeth or wash her face and hands without splashing water on herself.

Mouth full of foam, Jillian pulled the toothbrush out and pointed it at her mom. "It's simple, Mom." She answered, "I bring the granola bars to the park after school."

Jillian spit into the sink. Grabbing a hand towel hanging at wheelchair height, she dried her mouth. "I have a friend there and we use them for our tea party."

"You starve yourself before school so you can have granola bar tea parties in the park!" Vivian almost shouted at her little girl. Vivian had pretty much never yelled at Jillian. She wasn't much of a yeller to begin with, but when her little girl was born with spina bifida, she promised herself she'd never show her baby any anger of any kind.

Jillian knew this. She smiled at her mom and said, "I'm sorry if I've upset you. Anyway, I like crackers better than the cruddy cereal they have at school. They won't let me put the milk on for myself and it always gets soggy by the time I wheel over to the table."

Jillian paused for a minute because thinking about the milk dispenser being so high she couldn't reach it irritated her. *Seriously,* she wondered, *how tough would it be to get a lower stand for the milk?*

After a moment Jillian snapped back to the topic at hand – once again feeling excitement about her mom's offer, "But if you would buy boxes of granola bars at the grocery store and let me take them to the park, that would rock!"

Vivian leaned back on the bathroom wall. "It would rock, would it?"

Jillian foisted her backpack onto her lap and started wheeling herself toward the front door. "Yeah, it would so rock. Four other little kids come to our tea parties now, and Priscilla breaks the granola bars into pretty tiny pieces to make sure everyone has some. A whole box! Boy, oh boy, we could each have our own, and Priscilla could keep the leftovers."

Vivian knew they didn't have time to finish this conversation before the van arrived to take Jillian to school. Vivian reached into her purse and took out a ten-dollar bill, "Promise me that you will have cruddy cereal for breakfast today AND buy enough granola bars for your friends. You do that and I'll get you a whole box on my way home from work tonight."

Jillian gently took the bill from her mom's hand and put it into the zipper compartment on the front of her backpack. "You have yourself a deal!" Jillian said, smiling at her mom.

Vivian bent down and kissed her daughter on the cheek.

"When we get home tonight I want you to tell me more about these tea parties and your friends who hang around in the park with you every afternoon," Vivian called after her daughter as she wheeled down the walkway.

"I'm glad to know you meet your friends there. But maybe you should have a sitter with you at the park," her mom added.

Jillian kept rolling but called back loud enough to be heard, "No, it's okay. My friend Maggie has a sitter there every time."

Vivian considered this for a moment and replied, "She keeps a good eye on you too, though? Right?"

The county bus driver had walked around the passenger side of the van and was lowering the lift for Jillian. Jillian heard her mom but didn't turn around. She just raised her arm and waved, "Yes Mom. Thanks Mom. I love you, Mom."

CHAPTER 4

Tea Party

When the bell rang, the twins grabbed their jackets and ran to the park as fast as their feet could carry them. The twins loved Tuesdays. Tuesday at 3:30 was High Tea Time at the park. Priscilla would have her broken old tea set sitting by the fountain even before they arrived. They didn't actually use the tea set. The broken pot had been glued together in about a dozen places when Priscilla found it. Its fine porcelain body - long ago shattered - no longer held liquid of any kind. But, like most things in Priscilla's world, it still looked quite lovely from a distance. Most of the pink and yellow flowers matched up pretty well, and served its purposes for show.

The teacups that matched the pot were never found. Whoever had put the old pot in the dumpster behind the senior center must have kept the cups or tossed them elsewhere.

One might think a tea party wouldn't work without cups. Not Priscilla and her friends. None of them cared. Jeff and Beth and the others would fill their water bottles at the drinking fountain and use them as though they had tea. The six of them – three other children went to the tea parties too – would imitate Priscilla after she pretend poured out the imaginary tea.

They'd pick up their water bottles, stick their pinkies out straight, bring the bottle lip gently to their own, and sip cautiously so as not to burn themselves on their phantom hot liquid.

Jeff fell back a little along the sidewalk and gently shoved his sister, "C'mon slow poke! It's tea party day!"

Beth turned halfway around and continued running backwards – which, of course, slowed her down. She giggled joyfully, "Hey stop shoving me. I know what day it is. But we don't have to rush. We're usually the first ones there anyway."

"Except for Jillian," Jeff corrected his sister as he so often did on just about any topic from math to monster trucks. "Jillian gets a ride from the county van, so she's generally unloaded and in her wheelchair chatting up Priscilla by the time we get there. I love Jillian, but I like being the first person to greet Priscilla. She always makes such a fuss. Like she forgot it was Tuesday – even though she's got that cracked tea pot out on the fountain waiting for us."

Beth slowed down, despite her brother's insistence that they hurry. She had a question for him, "Do you think Jillian has the granola bars? I have some cheese and crackers that

Mrs. Tarrant gave us before we left school. We could share those if Jillian couldn't get them."

Jeff stopped running. In fact, he stopped walking all together. He reached his arms around his twin sister, pulling her in for a hug. At first it felt a little awkward to stand on the sidewalk hugging, but Beth's arms rose up and she held her brother close. After a minute or so, Jeff let go and looked at his sister with the seriousness of a much older boy.

Jeff spoke, "She'll have them. Don't worry. Even if she doesn't, we'll all have our water bottles, so we can still have a tea party. I want to share too, but if we don't bring Mrs. Tarrant's food home, we won't have anything for dad."

Beth nodded in agreement.

The twins began walking again – this time with a little less spring in their steps. Beth felt bad for suggesting they give away the food her teacher had given them. She wanted the gloomy moment to end, so she reached over, pulled her brothers shirttail and yelped, "C'mon slow poke, I'm gonna beat you to the park." Then she let go of his shirt and took off running.

Sure enough, when they arrived huffing and puffing like fairy tale wolves, Jillian had Priscilla's full attention. She also had a full box of granola bars on her lap in her chair.

Priscilla turned to look at the twins, "Well, if it ain't the little runners. Welcome to the tea party Count Jeff and Countess

21

Beth, we're thrilled to have you." Then she pointed to Jillian's lap, "Look what Lady Jillian brought to court today! Have you ever seen such bounty collected in just one week?"

The Count and Countess took turns bending fully at the waist. One after the other they pretended to kiss Priscilla's out stretched hand. "Princess Priscilla, 'tis an honor to be back in court for Tuesday Tea," Beth cooed.

Priscilla smiled at Beth's use of a new word, "'tis 'tis it?" Priscilla continued smiling, "Well, 'tis always my honor to have such fine subjects to share our stately realm."

Just then Vinny, a street musician who always sat far away enough not to disturb teatime – but close enough to be heard – started playing. When Vinny played in front of the post office he usually played guitar. But for Tuesday Tea he strummed his mandolin.

Priscilla looked over at Vinny and nodded to show her pleasure. He nodded back, took his ball cap from his head and with a sweeping gesture of his arm that went from high in the air down to the ground, he brushed his hat along the pavement. The park minstrel's grand gesture signaled to Priscilla that he was equally pleased to play.

No sooner had the music started then Tomas strolled up to the fountain. He had already peeled his backpack off so that he could take his water bottle from the side pouch. Excited as the rest of them Tomas shouted, "I remembered my tea cup this week!"

"Ahem," Priscilla cleared her throat.

"Oh gosh, I forgot." Tomas spoke again, this time remembering his form, "I remembered my teacup this week, Your Highness."

Priscilla smiled a smile that lit the entire park.

"Priscilla, the Princess of the Park! I come to ask a favor in your royal land." Priscilla, the twins and Tomas all looked past the fountain and watched Magdalena stroll forward, stopping every two or three steps to curtsy.

Pausing at every other seam in the concrete, Magdalena pulled at the sides of her jeans and scooted down in a squatting little bow. Magdalena had something wrapped around her shoulders that slid down over one elbow or the other with each of her faltering genuflections. The wrap was – of course – pink and purple and appeared festooned with hundreds of feathers.

As she grew nearer she proclaimed, "Priscilla, Princess of the Park, my peasant parents took me to the store last night, and I found these strands of feathers. Would you do me the honor of wearing them today at tea?"

Priscilla wrinkled her nose at Magdalena's comment. And though still smiling, Priscilla's eyes softened as she replied, "So Duchess

23

Maggie, have you been reading about medieval times? I'm excited about your expanded vocabulary, but I'm afraid your new word, "peasant" offends my royal ears. We are all mere peasants every second we are out of the park and away from each other. Our friendship makes us noble, but there is nothing noble about calling the people who love us unworthy names."

Tomas spoke up, "I like being called 'a noble peasant.' Can she call her parents that?"

Priscilla pondered the request, then answered, "That entirely depends on how she means it. Are they our equals? As all humans are. Then we may all call ourselves noble peasants."

Undeterred by the slight scolding and ensuing discussion, Magdalena handed the six purple and pink boas to her Princess of the Park. "Okay, forgive me. Please accept these gifts, for they are for you, M'lady," Maggie curtsied quite confidently this time.

Priscilla turned her attention to the boas, "Well, these are very festive. Thank you Maggie for thinking of us while you shopped with your parents. Yes, I do think at the correct time during our tea party, perhaps while Vinny plays a particularly formal tune, I shall decorate you all with your new royal trimmings." Vinny winked at the kids and they all smiled with anticipation.

Priscilla looked at the children she loved so well and said, "But first, and one at a time, why don't you tell me about how today went. Don't forget before we pass to the next person, you must each tell me at least one thing you enjoyed learning about today. Then I have a surprise for you."

Tomas blurted out, "I already know I liked learning that we're all noble peasants."

Priscilla shot him a sharp glance, and Tomas continued, "But I'll wait my turn." Tomas went first last time. They always went in alphabetical order. When Tomas spoke the week before – the end of the line for this little group – it signaled that the circuit would start over again. Every kid in Priscilla's court knew it.

Beth told the others about her day. Little Sherwood McGinnis brought her a flower from his mom's garden. Her lively story gave way to the next. Jeff, Jillian, Maggie and so forth.

The indulgent little children listened intently as they each spoke to the others. Sometimes they asked questions by raising their hand. Only the person speaking could acknowledge the would-be questioner. Not even Priscilla could interrupt the person speaking. Priscilla also took her turn talking about her day. She often spoke of the animals or plants that lived in the park. It was Tomas' favorite part of the game.

CHAPTER 5
Kenny Gets Home

Kenny always parked in the furthest spot away from the employee door at work. His car was so far away, he couldn't see it from the top of the loading dock stairs. He never worried about finding it, though. Most days he just walked toward the sound. He could hear his tinny front door speakers cranking out some overmodulated tune.

As he approached the first turn at the end of the line of his co-workers' cars, the music just got louder. Kenny smiled to himself, thinking, "The twins must have all the windows open and the radio cranked full blast."

Kenny walked by the trucks doubled up along the loading dock. When he stepped around the last one, he saw his goofy kids dancing in the vacant spaces next to their old Volkswagen.

Jeff and Beth held each other's hands and twirled around and around to the beat of Pinkfong's *Baby Shark*. Coincidentally, they were singing the part about the daddy shark as Kenny walked up, unnoticed, to meet them. Kenny disliked the song. He'd heard it about a million times. But he loved watching the kids sing it together. Besides, he couldn't help but grin when he heard the daddy shark lyrics. The words gave him yet another excuse to open his arms up wide and chase his kids around until he caught them in a big shark mouth kind of hug.

Kenny spoke loudly to be heard over the radio, "Well, I can tell it's Tuesday! You two are in particularly good moods."

"Dad!" The twins hollered in unison as they let go of each other and rejoined their hands around their father's waist.

Ken took his children's affection full force. The love attack knocked him backward a couple of steps. Still holding on, with his face muffled a little in his dad's T-shirt, Jeff spoke, "We got dinner for tonight. Mrs. Tarrant gave us cheese and salami and crackers. Then Priscilla surprised us with a bag of cucumbers. One of the farmers from the Monday Market dropped off his leftovers to her last night after they closed the stand. She remembered that you love cucumbers. So she asked us to share them with you."

Kenny stooped down and knelt on one knee. Now eye-level with his children he said, "Yum, that sounds delicious. I hope you remember to tell all these good folks how much your dad appreciates their kindness."

Beth started with an eye roll and finished by saying, "Of course we do, Dad. Mrs. Tarrant knows you're trying to save for the security deposit and first month's rent and that eating out in diners keeps eating into that." Beth giggled some more, "See what I did there. It's called a pun. Priscilla uses them all the time. Eating out – EATS into our savings – get it?"

Kenny stood back up and ruffled both kids' hair. Now it was his turn for an eye roll, "I get it. Pretty punny there, Beth. How come you always gobble up the good lines?"

The three of them groaned in unison.

Ken opened the driver's side door and got into the car, "C'mon you scavengers, let's see if there's enough juice in the battery to start this old clunker after your little dance party. We need to find out before Mr. Craig, the shop foreman, leaves with his jumper cables."

This would not have been the first time Mr. Craig had to jump-start Ken's car. Luckily it was Tuesday though, and the twins had spent so much time at the park with Priscilla and their friends, they hadn't listened to the radio very long. Beth and Jeff only had to wait in the parking lot an hour for their dad's shift to end.

To the twins every day would be better if every day were a Tuesday. Jeff and Beth liked Tuesdays because of tea parties and because they seldom sat in the car at all after the tea parties ended. Between the lengthy after school story shares and tea party snack hour, their visits with Priscilla lasted straight up to Ken's quitting time.

Ken put his hand on the ignition and turned the key to start. *Vroom*, the Volkswagen kicked to life. Ken tapped the dashboard, "Hop in kids, Martha's ready to take us to the PetroMart. Let's go get our showers and then we can find a quiet place to picnic on this feast you brought. With any luck we'll be able to park at Nilan National Park for the night."

Jeff and Beth buckled themselves into the backseat.

Ken continued, "Did either of you get a book to read this evening or do you two have too much homework?"

Beth, full of answers, replied, "We have a little math, but that won't take long."

Jeff piped up with a book choice. "How about tonight we start King Arthur and the Knights of the Round Table?"

"Excellent choice." Ken beamed at his children – one after the other – in the rearview mirror. "That's a great story. I have no doubt the Princess of the Park recommended it."

"Yup," both kids answered as one. Then Kenny turned the wheel. The Volkswagen motored onto the main street and headed for their favorite highway rest stop - the one that offered half price showers on Tuesday nights.

CHAPTER 6
Waiting for the Bus

Jillian didn't mind waiting for the bus alone. It never took terribly long. The trip home went more quickly than the ride to school ever did. Once the bus arrived, her afternoon attendant – a high school kid named Janelle - buckled her wheelchair into the appropriate space in the handicapped van twice as fast as the morning guy ever did.

Even though she felt chill about waiting by herself, Jillian never sat alone when she left the park. Tomas, his brother, Hugo, Maggie and her baby sitter, Lani – and often the sitter's boyfriend Charlie – all stood beside her until she got packed up and driven away. All good kids, they would have waited with her even if Priscilla didn't remind them each and every time they left the park. But Priscilla never took any chances that Jillian might sit by herself, "Tomas and Maggie, your parents make sure there's someone to get you home, so you do the same for Jillian," Priscilla would say.

Tomas and Hugo never told Priscilla that their parents didn't technically make sure Tomas got home from the park. They knew better. Their parents had no idea that they dawdled at the park. They knew their parents would pitch a full-blown fit if they had the slightest clue how long their boys hung out at the park – that's why their homework pact was such a flawless cover. Their folks and their grandmom, Bela, just assumed they were staying after school to work on Hugo's math problems.

Maggie reached over and started braiding Jillian's hair. "When we noble peasants were at the dollar store, I got some new hair ties. I have a pretty black one what would look amazeballs in your hair but will hardly show up in mine. Mind if I tie it on the end of your braid?"

Jillian smiled, "Knock yourself out, Lady Maggie. I love it when you play with my hair." Jillian sat up a little more stiffly in her wheelchair while the park's royal hairdresser did her work.

Maggie kept talking, "When you showed up with a whole case of granola bars – that floored me. Where'd you get a whole box?" Maggie rushed through the question without waiting for an answer. "You're lucky Priscilla didn't ask more questions, like, 'Are you going to get in trouble for taking those from school?' But now that we're waiting for the bus. I got to ask. Did you take those from school?"

Jillian giggled as she pictured the heist in her mind. Rolling up to Miss Camilla, the lunch lady that runs the register, with a whole box of contraband stuffed under a sweater on her lap. Miss Camilla would have smelled a rat right away and made her move the sweater. Then Jillian would have been busted for sure! She'd have had to make a break for it!

Smirking at Maggie she replied, "I can see the school newspaper headline now. *Girl in Wheelchair Rolls Away from the Scene of the Crime*. Although I do admit, with all those ramps at school, I could outpace anyone chasing after me."

Both girls giggled.

Tomas and Hugo stopped talking and began listening to the girls' far more interesting conversation about stealing granola bars from the cafeteria lunch lady. Jillian decided to share her granola secret with the others – before their imaginations made the story grow any larger in their minds. "I had to tell my mom today. She kind of figured it out anyway. Someone flagged her down at school and told her that I'd been skipping meals and buying granola bars instead. So I told her about our little tea parties."

Hugo nearly shouted, "You did WHAT?"

Tomas shushed him and said, "What do you care, Hugo? You don't even go to the tea parties."

Hugo whipped around and glared at his brother, "Which knight of the court are you again? Sir Dopey?"

"Hey, no hurting words," chimed in Lani, Maggie's sitter.

Hugo ignored the reprimand and just kept right on talking,

"Look Jillian, your mom might not mind if you hang out in the park with some scruffy old homeless lady, but let me tell you – in no uncertain terms – our parents, not to mention our Bela, will flatten us. They'll flatten me twice. Once for letting Tomas go and then again for not telling them."

Tomas just couldn't help himself. He balled up his fist and punched his brother right in the arm.

"Hey," Hugo yelled putting his hand on his brother's forehead and keeping him at arm's length, "Don't start something you can't finish."

Everyone looked over at Tomas. They watched his eyes fill with tears.

Maggie dropped Jillian's braid and put her arms around Tomas. Hugo let go of his younger brother's head. Jillian unlocked her wheelchair and turned it around to face her friend's brother. She looked up at Hugo and – in a voice borrowed from her mom's I'm-not-angry repertoire for speaking – asked him a very pointed and direct question, "In what universe is it okay to say something that mean about Priscilla or anyone in the park? Or anyone, period?"

Jillian's scolding had no effect on Hugo. In fact, he doubled down on his reality check for the tea partiers. "What's wrong with you little kids? You do know you're hanging out with a homeless lady, don't you? I'm not being mean. I'm just stating the facts."

Jillian's ride pulled up to the curb. Lani let go of Charlie's hand and took Maggie's instead. Then Charlie took Maggie by the other hand. Hugo started to feel like the others were ganging up on him – just for telling the truth. Hugo tried to turn his attention to his brother, but Tomas ran away from him in the direction of their apartment complex.

As the van driver lowered the lift to accommodate Jillian's chair, Jillian called after them, "My mom's okay with all of this. We don't need to fight about it. She told me she'd pick the granola bars up after work but then surprised me at school with them. She called me out of science class to give them to me."

Jillian felt awful that she and her friends had lost their cheerfulness. She yelled more loudly, "My mom is going to give us snacks for the tea party every week. She said she'd change them up, too." Now Jillian was full on shouting, but just so her dispersing friends could hear her, "Because she lives in a universe where kindness is more important than name calling." As the lift slowly raised Jillian and her chair into the air, Jillian whispered to herself, "Sometimes I think my mom invented that universe."

Janelle had climbed up the stairs at the front of the bus and waited for her inside. Jillian felt better when she looked into her attendant's caring face. "Janelle, you live in the kindness universe too, don't you?" Janelle smiled at the compliment and nodded. Then she fastened the harness on Jillian's wheelchair, and the bus pulled away.

CHAPTER 7

Lords, Ladies and Laundromats

Beth and Jeff had no idea that Hugo had shattered the crystalline good vibes they left the park with that afternoon. For all Beth and Jeff knew – their friends and Priscilla herself – were as happy as they felt in the afterglow of the day's events. They certainly would have been stunned into melancholy to learn that all the fuss had come about because Hugo has used the term "homeless" as an insult.

The twins sat together at the laundromat folding counter playing tabletop football using their hands for goal posts and a folded piece of paper for a ball. They'd finished their math homework. They'd filled their tummies with countless cucumber and cheese sandwiches. Freshly showered, they waited for their clothes to come out of the dryer so they could head over to the Nilan National Park and get some sleep.

Kenny looked over at his kids – patiently playing with each other – and he wondered if the twins were happy, or if they'd just gotten good at acting that way. Kenny hadn't wanted to do laundry that night but the hamper – aka the floor of the Volkswagen's backseat – had filled to overflowing, and he

knew the kids would appreciate some leg room. Besides, if the twins wore the same clothes to school too many days in a row, somebody might start asking questions.

The teachers thought the little Kritzell family was still doubled up. Ms. Pitzi, the school counselor, kept track of the kids without homes of their own. She thought Ken Kritzell and Beth and Jeff shared some living space at the twins' Uncle Mike's house.

Truth be told: Mike had kicked them out less then a week after they moved in with him and his wife, Gertrude. Seems Aunt Trudy wasn't as crazy about kids as she'd led them all to believe.

Trudy liked long baths. The kids constantly wanted to use the mobile home's one bathroom. The laundry piled up in the spare room – much like it would later collect on the floor of Martha the Volkswagen – and Trudy told the kids that it stank. Jeff and Beth thought Trudy's cigarettes stank, but they never told her that because they could tell she didn't much like them being around.

One night Ken fell asleep out on the couch watching TV. Uncle Mike and Aunt Trudy had a TV in their room and Trudy retreated there as soon as the kids came home from school each day. When Mike got home, he'd join her. So Ken stayed out on the couch and left the kids in the spare room by themselves. On this one particular night, Beth got up to use the bathroom and accidentally walked into her aunt and uncle's room in the dark.

Trudy got furious. She started yelling, "Those kids are always underfoot. They have no manners! What's she doing barging into our room? I want them all out. Now!"

It was almost six months earlier and after 10 p.m. when Trudy pitched her little hissy fit – as the twins called it – a term they proudly attributed to Priscilla. The Princess of the Park gave them daily vocabulary lessons that lent color and expression to their speech.

After the hissy fit and in the pitch dark, Ken loaded his pajamaed kids into the Volkswagen. The three of them drove to Nilan National park, pulled behind a grove of trees and slept there for the night.

Summers in college, Ken had been a janitor at Ohio's David Berger National Monument, so he knew that local law enforcement had no jurisdiction on national lands. Tiny national parks like Nilan and Berger also had no regular park rangers, so no one would make a person leave in the middle of the night. If someone or some family decided to sleep there, they could stay undetected until morning.

Once a week a National Parks truck would drive through and empty the trash cans and fill the toilet paper dispensers in Nilan's two restrooms. Years back the bathrooms got locked up at dusk and reopened at sunrise, but budget cuts eliminated the ranger who did all that locking and unlocking. Government belt tightening meant the Kritzells even had bathrooms to use at Nilan each night. A bathroom without a hissy fit! Beth told her brother and her dad that she'd sleep in a car every night if it meant that they could use a bathroom without making Aunt Trudy angry. So that's what they did.

Ken absentmindedly sorted clean clothes while staring at his children. Suddenly he came to attention. He had begun folding what looked to him like a tablecloth. It'd been a long time since the Kritzell family had a table, so he knew it wasn't theirs. Big and round and covered with bright colors, Ken stretched the cloth high over his head and asked, "What in blue blazes is this thing? Someone put a tablecloth in our wash basket."

Beth and Jeff turned to their dad. Ken stood completely obscured by the garment he held. The twins squealed with delight. Jeff kidded his dad, "That's no tablecloth silly, that's Priscilla's princess skirt."

"What in blue blazes are we doing with it?" Ken said blue blazes a lot when he wanted the kids attention but didn't want to sound angry.

Ken chuckled along with his kids. At that point, he poked his head through the waist of the gigantic circle of fabric.

Beth piped up this time, "We brought some of Priscilla's things home with us to wash. There should be a few pairs of socks in there and a sweater. Don't worry, Priscilla washes her own undies in the sink at the square. At first she didn't want us to help her. But we told her we go to a laundromat anyway, and it would be fun to help. She named us the Lord and Lady of the Laundry."

Ken made a goofy face and let the skirt settle down around his shoulders. "How come I'm the one doing the laundry and you're the guys who get the titles? Typical royalty. Let the peasants do all the work while you get all the glory."

Beth frowned deeply at her father and crossed her arms over each other against her chest.

Her dad looked shocked. "Why are you giving me that look?"

Beth said, "Priscilla says we are not to use the word peasant for each other. Priscilla says we're all equal and the only kind of peasant is a noble peasant. No one is any better than anyone else."

All of a sudden Ken's hands came out from under the skirt he'd draped over himself and he flung a sweater at Beth, "Okay, Lady Noble Peasant of the Laundry, you can fold her sweater!"

Jeff laughed and held his sides then, "Whoop!" a pair of socks came flying his way. "I know, I know," he chuckled. "The Lord of the Laundry gets to fold the royal socks."

44

CHAPTER 8

Brothers Need Each Other

H ugo must have apologized ten times if he apologized once. Even though he didn't really know what he'd done wrong, Hugo just hated having Tomas so mad at him.

Tomas made it home from the park a full three minutes before Hugo got there. That had never happened before. Hugo, bigger and faster, always beat Tomas at everything that required strength or speed. So yeah, Hugo let Tomas win. Hugo figured his little brother needed to blow off some steam. As Hugo approached he could see that his plan had failed. Tomas still had plenty of steam left.

Bela walked up to the door just as Hugo arrived. Bela had adjusted to the boys' new homework schedule, and she enjoyed a little more time out of the apartment on study days. Bela took a more relaxed approach to running errands. She even stopped at her favorite bodega most afternoons while the brothers did their math.

The boys' grandmother could tell by the heated look on Hugo's face and the icicles forming on Tomas cold stare that the boys had been arguing. "What is it with you two?" Bela asked, "You help each other and then you get mad at each other. Why don't you just stick to helping each other? Tomas, if you keep that angry look on your face it will freeze that way. I can see the frost forming already."

Neither boy would ever be rude to their Bela. For a few moments they stood there silent.

Hugo spoke first, "I'm sorry, Bela. It was my fault."

"Wowzie, wow wow," the grandmother imitated one of their exclamations. "Hugo, you must have done something pretty awful if you're admitting it this easily. I think you'd better find a way to make amends."

Then she turned to Tomas. "You two are lucky to have each other. I'm sorry Hugo made you so mad, but I know one thing about arguments. They are almost never all one person's fault. I don't want to know what happened. You children are getting bigger, and I don't need to know every detail. Unless one of you got physically hurt, then I would expect you to tell me. Tomas, you think about what part you might have played in this disagreement and then forgive your brother. You need each other and if you're good to each other, you'll always have each other."

Bela turned and waved to the doorman to let him know she was ready to enter the apartment building. "You know some families let each other down. I don't want you two to grow up that way." Bela had no way of knowing about Jeff and Beth and Uncle Mike, but she may as well have. Bela understood people and that's all it took to understand how families can go wrong.

Bela stepped through the door, "I'll go upstairs and start dinner. You come on in when you feel like it."

In an instant Bela was gone. Hugo looked at Tomas. "You can't stay mad at me forever. Can you?"

Tomas started to cry. All that steam had cooled and turned to water on his cheeks. He pulled a handkerchief from his pocket. He'd carried one ever since he could walk. His grandpa had always had his with him. Tomas started copying him at a young age. Tomas had a feeling he was the only person born in the 21st century that carted a cloth handkerchief around in his pocket. He didn't know why people stopped carrying handkerchiefs. They sure came in handy.

Tomas wiped his eyes and blew his nose. "Bela is right. It's not all your fault. It's mine too for having a secret and making you keep it." Tomas continued, again wiping his eyes, "You said such awful things about Priscilla, and you called her homeless. But you just see her the way Mama and Papa would. Maybe that made me angriest of all. If I told the truth to Mama and Papa, I'm afraid they would make me stop spending time with her. I'm not just mad at you. I'm mad at them too."

Hugo grabbed the handkerchief from his brother's hands, "Give me that snot rag! Now I gotta blow my nose."

Tomas smiled at the word: snot. Snot. Snot is just one of those words that could make the saddest angriest person smile – at least a little bit.

"Ew," Tomas whined. "You keep it now. I'll get a clean one upstairs."

The boys waved to the doorman. Once inside, Tomas raced into the elevator to press the up button. Hugo – feeling a little more like an older brother and a little less like Tomas' constant rival – just followed behind him. Again, he let him win.

After the elevator doors closed and they began their ascent to the 25th floor, Hugo said, "I'm afraid to ask this question because I don't want you to get mad again. But what are we going to do about that friend of yours who blabbed to her mom about the homeless lady– uh –Priscilla and the fact that you guys hang out with her in the park?"

"Jillian?" Tomas replied. "I don't know. It's a good question, but I have a headache now and I'm too scared to think about it. I wasn't scared when I was mad at you. Maybe I do want you to make me mad again."

The elevator doors were opening and Hugo said, "Well I could punch you!"

Hugo laughed loudly and ran for their apartment door.

CHAPTER 9
Treasured Secrets

Magdalena stayed in her room even after her mother called her to come down for dinner. She settled down into the pillows on her pink and purple bed, turning the metal clasp Priscilla had given her over and over in her hands.

The argument between Hugo and Tomas didn't upset her too much. Those two bickered all the time. No, what upset Magdalena was the word Hugo used. Homeless.

Magdalena never thought about using that word for Priscilla. Now she couldn't stop thinking about it. Homeless. Didn't Priscilla have a home? Where did she go after the kids left the park? Magdalena assumed she pushed her little walker to the bus stop, or called a cab. But she and the other kids had never seen her leave the area by the fountain or the bench Priscilla called her throne.

Magdalena felt sick to her stomach. The bags of items neatly tucked under the bench, were those Priscilla's blankets? Thinking back on them, they looked like blankets. Could it be true that Priscilla had nowhere to live? What about the park? If she had blankets under her throne, did that make the park her home?

Downstairs, Shewan and Gabriel chopped vegetables for a salad. Magdalena loved salad and she loved salmon, so her parents agreed that something must be bothering their daughter if she stayed upstairs even after they told her that dinner was downstairs waiting.

"Maybe you should go and get her," Shewan told her husband. "Maybe you can find out what's eating at her."

Gabriel put down the paring knife and dried his hands on the dishcloth. He kissed his wife on the cheek and headed to the front of the house.

Once at the bottom of the stairs, Gabriel shouted in a deep

voice, "Fe Fi Fo Fum, I'm coming to tell you that dinner is done." He said it over and over, clomping his feet on the stairs and chanting like a giant crossing to the other side of a beanstalk.

Magdalena didn't budge. She knew the routine. Gabriel would act all giant-like when he got to her room. Then when she didn't get up or move, he'd pluck her from where she was sitting and toss her over his shoulder to take her downstairs. Even though Magdalena was getting bigger every day, Gabriel figured he had a few good years left of being able to carry her to the dinner table.

When Gabriel hurled her over his shoulder this time, Magdalena pretended not to notice that a giant had taken her. As Maggie swung through the air, she dropped what she'd been holding. Something fell on the floor behind them. It was the metal clip Magdalena had been flipping around in her hands. Gabriel turned around to see what had fallen. Gabriel squatted down gently, his daughter slung over his shoulder like an important parcel he didn't want to drop. Picking up the clip, Gabriel asked – still using his giant voice – "Fe Fi Fo Fum, did you drop this? 'Cause it bounced off my bum."

Magdalena finally chuckled. "Yeah, it's the little clip that Priscilla gave me last week. I showed it to mom, but she thinks Priscilla is my imaginary friend. So she didn't pay it much attention. She said it's just some broken piece of a watch or something. She thinks I found it on the ground and that I'm pretending it's a gift from Priscilla."

Gabriel turned the clip around in his hand.

"Uh, Dad," Magdalena gurgled. "Could you put me down while you look at that. The blood is rushing to my head."

Gabriel slowly crouched down and placed his daughter on her feet. Magdalena pulled herself upright.

"Maggie, this looks like the clasp from a Rolex watch. See that little crown there? That's their logo." Gabriel had solved the mystery, even if the person who gave it to his daughter still seemed incomprehensible to his wife.

"Yeah, it probably is. Priscilla salvages stuff from the park trash cans all the time. She has this wacky teapot that we use for tea parties. It's all broken, like this clasp. But I don't care. She gave this to me because it has that crown on it there. See, she's the…"

Her dad cut her off. "She's the princess of the park."

Gabriel continued, "You know, Maggie. I think this is real gold. It's probably worth a few bucks. Perhaps if Priscilla's real, you should give it back to her."

Magdalena frowned, "You don't believe she exists either, do you?"

Gabriel looked down and shrugged. "Does it really matter as long as you're enjoying the experience?"

Magdalena's dad was right about one thing. It didn't matter what her parents thought. Maggie knew Priscilla, knew her quite well actually and their friendship meant the world to her.

Magdalena thought a little more about the clasp, "Dad, do you really think it's worth something? Because I'll give it back if it is. I'm pretty sure you're right. Priscilla could use a few bucks."

Gabriel bent over and picked his daughter up again. This time not as a giant and this time he held her right side up. He kissed her cheek and whispered in her ear, "Let's go downstairs and eat that yummy dinner that's waiting for us. It's your favorite. We're having salmon."

Magdalena hugged his neck and kissed his cheek too. When he put her down, she rushed over to her box of keepsakes and dropped the clasp in with her other treasures. She had a pigeon feather, some rocks that she and Priscilla and the other kids had colored with chalk. Magdalena also had all the fifty-cent pieces her parents gave her every time they came across one shopping or at the bank. Oh, and her Great Grandma Harriet's hairpins. She saved those because they mattered to her dad. The same reason she kept her long hair.

The clasp was safe, dinner was delicious and Priscilla was no more real to Gabriel or Shewan than she'd ever been.

Maggie smiled to herself as she sat with her folks in the kitchen. Hugo might have worried about grown-ups learning about Priscilla. *But*, Magdalena thought, *He doesn't need to worry about my parents – they don't have a clue.*

The clasp and the secret of the lady who lived in the park were both safe.

CHAPTER 10
The Trouble Makers

Jillian grabbed both armrests on the electronic chair at the grocery store. Then she took a deep breath and pushed herself out of her wheelchair landing squarely on the seat of the GrocerCar2000. Vivian smiled watching her daughter navigate the transition from her own chair to the supermarket's public accommodation for the physically handicapped. No, Jillian didn't need to use the motorized cart, but she loved driving it. She also liked being able to select her own groceries and place them in the vehicle's front basket.

"Mom, do you ever want to drive the GrocerCar2000?" Jillian loved the cart's name. The plaque on the side of the motor read GrocerCar2000 and when Jillian first read that it made her giggle. Now she used the cart's name every chance she got. Half the time she spoke about it, she sounded like a commercial for some joyride gizmo. Jillian often said in her most announcer-like voice, "Seriously Mom, the GrocerCar2000 is a thrilling ride through the grocery maze." Then in a voice a little more kid-like, "I can let you use it if you want some day. Just to see how fun it is."

Vivian waved the offer away by wagging her fully extended hand. "No thanks, little missy. After watching your dad nearly take out the oranges display when he tried, I'll stick to walking beside you if that's all right."

Jillian felt a little proud of that fact that at eight years old she could drive pretty much anything with a motor. Jillian's parents had taken her go-cart racing before most kids had their training wheels off their bicycles. Jillian grinned a self-congratulatory if-you-say-so smirk at her mom and pulled away from the wall.

Jillian moved the GrocerCar2000 slowly so her mom could keep up while walking by her side. "Jillian, remind me to get cat food when we get to the pet aisle. I've been feeding Toby human tuna fish for the last two days, and while I'm sure she doesn't mind – it's a bit expensive."

"Okay, Mom," Jillian chirped. The pair turned down the first aisle of the grocery store. Oversized packages lined both sides of the walkway. Vivian usually avoided shopping in that section because every package had enough to feed an army. But now there were tea parties to supply and Vivian figured the larger packages would make providing many snacks easier if not less expensive.

"Tell me, Jillian." Her mom asked, "Do you even like granola bars? Or do you just get them because it's all they sell at school that you can keep wrapped up in your backpack until you get to the park? There are all kinds of other things we can get. See? There are cheese crackers. Packages of peanuts. Oh, wait. Do any of the other kids have peanut allergies?"

Jillian shook her head – her blonde braid with Maggie's black scrunchy slapping her back and forth across her shoulders as she did. "I don't see how anyone could have an allergy. We've never been the least bit worried about the ingredients list on the granola bars. My food science teacher says that just about every kind of junk food is made with peanuts or peanut oil. But none of us have ever gotten sick."

Vivian frowned. "Okay," she responded, "I'm just worried. But I worry about everything. You know what else I'm worried about?"

Jillian sent her braid whipping across her shoulders again.

Vivian answered her own question, "I worry that your friend Priscilla doesn't have anywhere to live."

The motorized cart stopped dead in front of an eight foot raisin display. "Oh, raisins! Can we get raisins, Mom? That'd be a nice change from granola bars."

Vivian pulled two raisin twelve packs off the display and handed them to Jillian who dropped them into the basket in front of her. Jillian squeezed the drive button on the handlebar and the mechanized grocery chair lurched forward.

"Did you hear me, Jillian?" Her mom called to her.

Jillian, now more than 10 feet from her mom, slowed the cart, looked back and said, "Yes, I heard you. Why are you standing there?"

Vivian didn't budge. "I'm standing here because I want you to talk to me." Vivian raised her hands to her hips and continued, "I think it's an important consideration and I don't like thinking about that poor woman – or anyone – having nowhere to go."

Jillian pulled the cart's handle bar back with her left hand and made a U-turn in the aisle. Then, staring at her mom, Jillian whispered, "Mom," she gestured with both arms circling the air, "Do you think this is any place for a discussion like that? What if someone hears you? There are people who don't know she sleeps in the park. Do we really need to have a conversation around so many people who might know what we are talking about and make some serious trouble for her?"

Vivian couldn't believe her ears. Just as she asked herself how her little girl might get so paranoid, Mrs. Shewell, the – hands down – nosiest neighbor in their town came around the corner. Jillian quickly changed the subject and her volume shouting, "Oh hi, Mrs. Shewell! Look, Mom. Behind you, it's Mrs. Shewell."

Vivian cringed. When her face returned to normal she twisted around from the waist up and waved.

Mrs. Shewell did what she always did when she saw people she hadn't seen in a while. She started with twenty questions that never were any of her business. After that, she launched into gabbing about one or another of their neighbors.

Never out of character, Mrs. Shewell chirped, "Well hello. Vivian. Hello Jillian. Jillian, are you old enough to drive that machine? Vivian, do you think it's a good idea for a little girl to operate machinery like that? I'm sure you cleared it with the store manager. You did, didn't you? I mean they have insurance premiums and I'm sure their insurance company wouldn't even consider paying for any damage done when a parent doesn't appropriately supervise her children…"

And she was off! On and on she went. Along about the time Mrs. Shewell accused Vivian of endangering everyone shopping at Safe Rite that day by letting her daughter drive the GrocerCar2000, Vivian twisted back around to face Jillian and started rolling her eyes and sticking out her tongue.

Jillian just sat quietly watching her mom make faces and listening to Mrs. Shewell make trouble.

Finally, their nosy neighbor took a breath. Vivian spoke up – loudly enough to be heard while talking back-to to their busybody companion, "Why actually Mrs. Shewell, that's why my husband, Edgar, doesn't come grocery shopping anymore. He's still recovering from the concussion he got when Jillian ran him over with the cart.

Jillian and Vivian both burst out laughing.

Mrs. Shewell, never put in her place by anyone, just kept right on muttering about danger. After a quick goodbye, Jillian and her mom sped away with their raisins, headed for the cash registers.

Once Jillian buckled the car's seat belt, Vivian loaded the wheelchair into the trunk. "Wow, I can't believe what a close call that was. You warned me about troublemakers and then bam! The nosiest, least-helpful person in the whole town comes walking into the bulk food aisle. I have to admit, though, it makes me quite sad that you are so aware of things like troublemakers. How does a young person even know that grown-ups could or might make trouble for Priscilla?"

Jillian thought back to the argument Hugo and Tomas had while waiting for the county bus earlier that same afternoon. Jillian, grateful for a mom to whom she could tell the truth, replied, "I'd like to say it's because I heard my friends arguing about whether or not Priscilla is homeless, but it's more than that."

Vivian kneeled down in the parking lot next to her daughter's open car door. She could see the joy leaving Jillian's face. "Oh, sweetie, I'm sorry. Tell me."

Tears rimmed Jillian's bright blue eyes. "Well," she spoke and her voice cracked as she did, "One day I got there super early because the county bus brings me to the park before the other kids get there, and I saw a man in green coveralls with the letters 'REC DEPT' pulling on the things that Priscilla keeps under her bench. I don't know where Priscilla had gone, but he was stuffing Priscilla's things into a humongous garbage bag. He almost got away with it too, but it was a Tuesday and just as he was pulling the last of her things out onto the sidewalk, Vinny, the street musician walked up and started yelling at him."

A tear fell down Jillian's cheek. "I'm so mad. I'm not crying because I'm a baby, Mom. I'm crying because I'm mad."

"I know," her mom choked on a few of her own tears too. "Please, Jillian, tell me what happened."

"Well, Vinny grabbed the bags from the man's hands. He told him to get lost and never come back. He told him if he ever tried anything like that again that he'd call the cops and have him arrested for stealing Priscilla's things."

Vivian whispered, "Next Tuesday I want to pick you up at the park, not the county bus. I want to meet Vinny. He sounds like a wonderful guy."

"He really is, Mom. He really is. Anyway, the guy from the park told Vinny to go right ahead and call the cops. He said the police would probably help him throw 'the old lady's stuff away' – that's what he called her – the old lady." Jillian's nose started dripping. Her mom searched for a tissue.

"I'll be there this Tuesday, Jillian. It's time I met Priscilla anyway. Sounds like she might need somebody to stick up for her. Somebody besides Vinny." Then Vivian kissed her daughter's forehead.

Jillian grabbed her mom around the neck, "Mom, I'm always glad you're my mom. I mean it. But today, I'm really, really glad."

CHAPTER 11

Thursday at the Park

T he county bus pulled away from Mitch Snyder
Elementary and Middle School and headed for the park.
Jillian carried her backpack full of raisins on her lap right
next to her stomach full of butterflies. Excited that it was
Thursday and another chance to see Priscilla and the park
posse. That's what her mom had started to call her collection
of friends. Jillian feared trouble. Truth be told, she'd been
scared ever since the guys who work for the town tried to
mess with Priscilla's things.

Vivian tried to make sense of it all
for Jillian. Vivian had explained to her
daughter that the letters REC DEPT
on the guys shirts meant Recreation
Department. The men basically worked
keeping the community public areas
clean and in working order. Watching
them try to take Priscilla's things and
then hearing the way Hugo spoke
about Priscilla worried Jillian.

How could people look at Priscilla and see her any other way from how the posse saw her? It confused Jillian entirely that anyone could see a nice old woman that surrounded herself with pretty things – even if they were salvaged from the dumpsters in town – and think *that lady's got to go*.

Jillian felt her face getting hot and her eyes swimming in tears. Janelle, her bus attendant, knew something bothered her little companion and said, "Hey, do you need me and Burt to stay at the park with you today? Or come back early?" Then Janelle turned to the bus driver and shouted, "Hey Burt, we just got one other pick up, right? Mr. Flynn needs a ride to physical therapy then we can come back and wait by the side of the park for Jillian. Can't we? I mean no reason to park in the county lot when the park is right there."

Burt's shoulders slumped listening to his bus attendant ask him to break the rules. He sighed. *Won't be the first time and won't be the last time* ran through his head. Burt managed a weak smile and said, "Sure, Janelle. Old man Flynn don't take too long. Maybe he'd even like to come to the park with us."

Janelle knew Burt kidded her to make the point that they were breaking rules again – so why not break them all and kidnap an old man and take him to the park. She got the point and then dismissed it. Her little Jillian had some heavy stuff on her heart and she wanted to be there for her.

Janelle looked at Jillian – the little kid sat clutching raisin snacks. Janelle reassured her friend, "I live in a universe where we stick together when somebody's upset. We'll get back from Mr. Flynn's appointment right away and just wait for you in case you need us."

64

Jillian smiled but not as broadly as she used to. She appreciated Janelle being in the good guy universe. But Jillian had begun paying better attention to the other universe. The one where Mrs. Shewell couldn't say a nice thing if her life depended on it. The one where maintaining the park meant throwing a woman's things away.

The bus pulled up to the park and Jillian wheeled herself over to the lift door. It was only Thursday. Her mom wouldn't be able to meet Priscilla for five more days – not until Tuesday. What if the men made Priscilla leave the park before then? Janelle lowered the lift with Jillian on it. When she rolled onto the sidewalk and looked up at her helpful friend, Janelle called down to her, "We got you on this. You just have fun. Enjoy your visit and we'll be back before you know it. Nobody's going to mess with our universe today."

CHAPTER 12
What's Your Major Malfunction?

Jillian rolled up beside Priscilla's bench, "Good afternoon, Your Highness." Priscilla greeted her young friend, "Why doth thou look so melancholy today? Did something happen in thy realm of education?"

Jillian smiled back, "Oh, it's nothing, fair Princess of the Park. How's your day going?"

Before Priscilla could answer, Beth and Jeff ran up to them. Beth grabbed Jillian's chair and spun it around shouting, "Time for park dancing!" Jillian giggled. It shocked her how good laughing felt. Jillian thought, *this is just what I need!* Priscilla sprang to her feet. The four of them – Jeff, Priscilla and Beth, who danced with Jillian's chair in her hands – boogied right there in the middle of the sidewalk.

"Princess Priscilla, tell us about when you were a dancer again," Beth pleaded. "I beseech thee, tell us of dancing in the royal court."

"Okay, just let me finish this little jig I'm doing. Do you remember how to jig?" Priscilla asked.

Of course! They all did. Beth and Jeff dropped their hands to their sides and displayed the fancy footwork Priscilla had taught them months earlier. Their form was quite good, and they danced for two minutes or so next to Priscilla when Tomas and Magdalena joined them. The five of them formed quite a line. They had cut off the footpath from walking traffic as Jillian twirled herself around in her chair. Then she rolled up on her chair's back two wheels and danced right along beside them.

Suddenly an older kid on a skateboard hollered and jumped off his board which shot off into the grass.

Hugo came out of nowhere and yelled at the kid, "Whoa Dude, what's your major malfunction?"

Everyone stopped dancing.

The boy with the skateboard stood up to Hugo's advance and said, "Don't yell at me, Dude. They're the ones dancing in the middle of the sidewalk. They don't even have any music so I didn't hear them. If I hadn't looked up when I did, I'd have plowed into that kid in the chair."

Hugo puffed his chest full of air. This kid with the skateboard was a few years older than Hugo, but Hugo knew he could handle him. Hugo said, "Well say you're sorry to the Princess and her dopey little friends and I'll let you get away with it this time."

The skateboarder bent over and picked up his board. He rolled his eyes at Hugo. Then turning to Priscilla and the little kids, he said, "Look lady, I'm sorry I nearly clobbered you all. But there's got to be a safer place to dance." Then he looked over at Hugo, "We good?"

Completely self-satisfied Hugo responded, "Yeah, we good."

After the ruckus ended. Priscilla asked everyone to sit and discuss what had happened. Beth, Jeff, Maggie and Tomas took their places on the grass near Priscilla's throne. Hugo started walking back to the tree where he stood waiting for his brother every Tuesday and Thursday afternoon.

"Not so fast, Hugo." When Priscilla called his name, Hugo stopped walking. "Why don't you join us for this conversation?"

"Nah, I'm good. You guys play your little fairy tale games. I'll just wait over there." Hugo pointed to his tree.

"Please, Hugo." Priscilla looked at the big boy and put her arms up in the air. "Please come sit with us. You're more and more a part of this group every day, whether you like it or not."

"I am?" Hugo asked.

Nobody said anything after Hugo asked his question. Hugo already felt bad that he'd yelled at the little kids and called Priscilla homeless. Priscilla inviting him to be part of the group somehow made him feel even worse.

Nope, Hugo pushed his feelings back, *I don't want to be caught dead hanging out with a bunch of little kids and some homeless lady in the park. Don't want any part of it.*

Hugo responded, "Nah, I'm okay. Thanks anyway."

"How about a compromise?" Priscilla suggested, "Just come over for one quick conversation and then when our Thursday afternoon UNO game starts, you can go back to your tree."

Finally Hugo agreed, "I'll come hear what you got to say, Princess, but I ain't sitting down."

With the exception of a few birds calling to each other and the water running over the side of the stone basin in the fountain, the park grew silent. Priscilla's posse – along with one reluctant young man on the fringe – stared at their favorite person. Priscilla looked into their eyes and said with a bright voice, "I've always believed that a little excitement will show who your true friends are. Did anyone learn anything new from our little run-in with the wild skateboard man?"

Tomas raised his hand.

Priscilla nodded to him and he spoke, "I don't think the guy on the skateboard was looking where he was going. But I don't think he wanted to hurt us either. He could have banged himself up pretty bad the way he jumped off and ditched the board into the grass like he did."

The others nodded then murmured in agreement.

Jeff's hand went up next.

Priscilla looked his way as he agreed, "Yeah, we were all pretty lucky. A bunch of us might have gotten clobbered if he hadn't stopped. Maybe we should dance on the grass from now on."

Beth chimed in, "But Jillian can't get up on two wheels on the grass. Jillian won't be able to dance."

Jillian's hand shot into the air.

Priscilla looked her way and Jillian spoke, "Let's use music next time. I mean, let's use music that's not in our heads. The guy said he would have known we were there if we'd had music. My phone plays music."

Priscilla smiled, "Well that's a good idea! Okay, from now on, by royal decree, and out of respect for the other subjects of the realm – dance parties shall hence forth and always have music everyone can hear."

Tomas started clapping his hands. "Hooray, the noble peasants shall have music!"

"Oh brother," sighed Hugo. "Was that what this was all about? Bringing your goofy kids – uh… subjects – together to come up with music at dance parties. Don't you guys think someone thought of it before you all did? Can I go back to my tree now?"

"Just one more minute, Hugo," answered Priscilla. "I realize music at dance parties is something you take for granted, but our little – what does your mom call us now, Jillian? Our little posse has been breaking out in spontaneous dances for a while now. Adding music will be very new. In the past, we only had Vinny playing background music at the tea parties. I think this is a wonderful new idea."

Hugo shifted his weight from one foot to the other. He looked unconvinced.

Priscilla ignored his impatience and continued, "I called a discussion meeting to solve the problem of dancing in the park. But that's not the only reason. I also wanted to discuss what we learned from the whole experience of that young man almost hurting himself and us. Did we learn anything?"

The little group studied each other as if a clue might be found on someone else's face.

A bird chirped. "Maybe that dumb bird knows the answer," Hugo quipped.

Then Tomas raised his hand, "I think I know."

Priscilla responded, "I thought you'd be the one to figure it out, seeing as you've had the most experience with this."

Tomas continued, "We learned that Hugo cares about us. Even though he calls us dopey or dumb. I mean, he just called that bird dumb – but birds know how to fly – that doesn't seem too dumb to me. But yeah, he saw that guy headed straight for Jillian, for all of us, and he came out of nowhere to save us."

All the little kids started saying, "Yeah," and "Hey, that's right," and "Thanks Hugo."

Hugo looked back at the little gathering. His jaw fell open while he processed what his brother had said. Then he quipped, "Cut it out will ya? What was I supposed to do, let some jerk smash into a bunch of little dopes dancing without music?"

Priscilla spoke next, "That was very brave of you Hugo. Although, heaven knows I'd love it if you'd use kinder language when talking to these little lords and ladies. But Tomas is right. You didn't think for one minute about yourself. You just leapt into action to help us. I am grateful, Hugo. I'm very grateful no one got hurt. Not the little kids and not the big boy on the skateboard. I'm so grateful that I am going to give you a title. You don't have to kneel on one knee but I really wish you would."

Then the whole posse chimed in together, "Oh Hugo, just play along. It'll be fun."

Hugo rocked his head back and forth. Again that little voice in his head told him to get as far away from this woman and these little kids as possible. But this time he ignored that voice. Hugo wondered what his title would be. Priscilla and the kids applauded loudly as Hugo bent one leg and settled down on his knee in the grass.

"Oh, crud," Hugo gasped, "The grass is wet. How about you weirdos get this over with as fast as possible."

Then Priscilla stood up and drew a long willow branch out from behind her bench. She raised the branch high over her head then brought it down gently to land on one of Hugo's shoulders and then on the other. While she brushed the shoulders of the young man kneeling before her, Priscilla proclaimed in a deep and formal voice, "I, Priscilla, the Princess of the Park, name you, Sir Hugo, the Protector of the Realm. I hereby command that all those subject to the throne, noble peasants that we are, recognize you for your bravery and quick reflexes in the face of danger – both seen and unseen. Please rise, Sir Hugo, the Protector of the Realm."

The little kids squealed with delight. Hugo bowed a little to Priscilla and then he did something that shocked them all, Hugo replied, "Thank you, Your Highness. This is quite an honor."

Jillian pushed the play icon on her phone and music stated blaring. She popped back on her two wheels and shouted, "Dance Party."

Hugo bowed again and then the Protector of the Realm
retreated to his spot by the tree.

CHAPTER 13

Ken Visits the Park

Ken pulled up beside the park. He knew the kids would be somewhere in there playing with Priscilla. He wanted to find them before they started walking over to the warehouse. He knew they'd be pleasantly surprised to see him – and he always enjoyed surprising them.

Ken couldn't believe his eyes when he saw the little crowd, five kids dancing with an older woman. She had festooned herself with brightly colored handkerchiefs hanging from her belt. A little girl in a wheelchair scurried around as fast as the kids on their feet. Behind them an older boy leaned against a tree looking very stern and watchful.

Gee, Ken thought, Priscilla really dresses the part. No wonder Beth and Jeff are so in love with her. As Ken looked closely, he could see the dirt along the hem of Priscilla's skirt. Her sweater had a few holes in the sleeves and her fingernails, partially covered with pink enamel, were cracked and grubby looking. Priscilla didn't exactly look grimy, but she didn't look clean either.

Ken, who knew living outside all too well, figured he knew her story too. He knew that without a car, Priscilla wouldn't be able to get to the truck stops he and the kids went to for their weekly showers. The Mission House, only a few blocks away would have demanded Priscilla comply with their rules to use the showers they provided to the poor. Priscilla had long before stopped obeying other people's rules. The fountain in the middle of the park had clean water. In case of an emergency, Priscilla could wash something off there. Under normal circumstances, Priscilla could take a sponge bath in the restroom sink anytime from sunrise to sunset.

Still, Ken thought, *What's our little old princess doing with herself in the middle of the night?*

This question bothered Ken. It bothered him a lot. He knew the twins loved her. This past week Ken had worked so much overtime that he volunteered to leave early one day. He didn't like to do that – leave early – because it interfered with his plan to get a home for himself and the kids. But Priscilla's situation upset him. He could lose a few hours pay to make sure she was okay.

Ken stood there – not fifteen feet from his own children for a full five minutes. Not one of the whirling performers noticed him. The big kid up by the tree gave him a few stern looks, Ken waved and Hugo nodded as if to say, Okay, buddy, but just so you know I have my eye on you.

Finally Ken shouted over the music, "Mind if I cut in?"

Beth and Jeff cheered, "DAD!" Their customary full on love attack ensued. Fully prepared for their affection assault, Ken barely budged.

Beth and Jeff, overjoyed at the sight of their dad in their favorite place with their other favorite people, spoke over each other trying to introduce him.

"This is our dad, this is our dad," the twins shouted. Ken said hello to each child in turn.

"Well, hello Jillian," Ken gushed. "I hear I have you to thank for my kids getting a great snack every Tuesday during the tea parties."

Perfectly polite, Jillian humbly responded, "Well, really my mom. But she's very happy to do it."

Ken then turned to Tomas, "Hi, Tomas. Is that big guy up at the tree yours? He sure looks like you."

Tomas beamed with pure pride, "Yup, that's my big brother, Sir Hugo. He's the Protector of the Realm."

HUGO

PROTECTOR of the REALM

"Ahhh," agreed Ken, "Well, I wouldn't mess with him. I'm glad to see he's on the job."

Ken felt a tug at his sleeve. Ken glanced down at the charming little girl with tightly curled black hair who still had one leg dancing while she introduced herself, "I'm Maggie. Your kids are very nice, Mr. Kritzell. It's really fun that you came to the park to meet us."

"It's a pleasure for me too, Miss Maggie," the twins' father replied.

After meeting the children and giving another wave to Hugo who had taken on a much less threatening posture, Ken moved over toward Priscilla. The Princess of the Park sat herself back down on her throne and prepared to meet the first parent that had taken the time to meet her.

While Hugo let his guard down, Priscilla had put hers up. She didn't know what any of the kids' parents would want from her if they actually met her. Every day Priscilla woke up with the full knowledge that some, or all, of the parents might not want their kids to visit with her in the park.

Ken put his arms out to either side. He swung his right arm in front of his stomach and his left arm behind his back. While swinging his arms he bent completely in half at the waist.

As Ken straightened out from his bow he spoke, "Your Royal Highness, Priscilla, the Princess of the Park, it is my great honor to present myself in your court. I am Ken, your humble driver of forklifts. I beseech you to allow me to address your court."

The kids jumped up and down and applauded Ken's fine courtly manners. Beth yelled, "Oh Dad, you are so funny. Priscilla, isn't my dad funny? He always plays along with us and now he's in the park."

Priscilla looked at all her little friends. Then she looked at Ken. "Welcome, Ken. To what does our court owe the honor of your visit? Are there no forklifts left to drive in the kingdom at this hour?"

Ken reached out and held Priscilla's hand in front of him. She looked genuinely startled. Then Ken bent down again and kissed her knuckle and said, "Alas, my lady, I have driven the beasts so much this week that my noble lord would have to pay me overtime. So I'm free to join the dance in the park."

With that Jillian turned her music back on and the group joined hands to spin in a great big circle. Round and round they went until Ken broke free and said, "I need a rest. I'm not as young as you little sprites. You keep dancing, I'm going to see if Priscilla has room for me near her on that throne."

The Princess of the Park begrudgingly moved aside and let Ken sit beside her. She leaned in and whispered to him, "I'm letting you sit here to make the twins happy. But I don't know what you want so why don't you tell me and then you can move on."

Ken nodded. "I'm not surprised you don't trust me. Honestly, I don't trust anyone either. Trust is a luxury neither one of us can afford in our current situations. So, seeing as I don't want you to know any more about me than you might already, let me just tell you that I don't want to know anything more about you either."

Priscilla liked what she heard so far. Ken was right. She didn't know much about Ken, except that the teachers sent food home with the kids – so she knew someone knew Ken and the kids had money trouble. That's why she gave the kids extra vegetables when she got them from the Monday Market.

Priscilla's voice and face changed in that moment. She didn't look like a pretend princess in fancy tattered clothes anymore. Suddenly – and maybe just to Ken – she looked like a tired old woman with a few anger issues. Ken took Priscilla's change in stride. He had a few things making him angry too.

"Look Ken, I'm glad you can keep quiet. Loose lips sink ships, after all. And I ain't got much of a ship here. So why don't you tell me what you came here to tell me." Priscilla stared at him, waiting for a response.

"The kids and I go to a truck stop up on the highway. Tuesday nights the showers are half price. Once a month there are some church folks who come and buy dinner for everyone in the parking lot." Ken looked over his shoulder and then back at Priscilla, "If you ever want to come with us, I'd be happy to pick you up after the tea party and you can tag along. I can bring you back here after."

The tired old woman spoke, "That's mighty kind of you, Ken."

Mighty kind but stupid, Ken thought.

Priscilla – the weary Priscilla that only Ken could see – continued, "I'm okay. I hope whatever has pulled your family into the world I live in lets go quick and you get back on your feet. The longer you're down, the further you get from ever getting your life back – so keep taking that overtime when your boss offers it.

"Another thing, Ken, I appreciate your offer. I do. But I'm going to turn you down. I don't dare leave my spot for 15 minutes around here, let alone a couple of hours. For all I know, you're one of those people that's been trying to get me out of the park for the last year and a half."

Priscilla studied Ken's face.

"No, I don't think you are one of them. I think you and your kids are the real deal. So I'll tell you what you can do for me." Priscilla licked her lips and Ken could see that a few of her teeth were missing. "I'll keep a good eye on your kids here in the park every day after school. It's nice here and we have fun. It's out in public and it's pretty much always safe. You let me look after your kids so you can do all the overtime your boss throws your way. Then you get yourself a place. That's what you can do for me, Ken."

Ken's heart was ready to burst with love and gratitude and sorrow for this old woman. He instinctively reached over and hugged Priscilla tightly to himself. Priscilla brought her willow branch up over his head and whapped him on the hair.

"Unhand me, you beast," cried the Princess of the Park. The kids squealed with laughter as they watched Priscilla pretend to pound on Jeff and Beth's dad. Even Hugo up at his tree laughed loudly at the display. Ken pulled back, playing along, with his arms folded in front of his face. When he brought his hands down, old weary Priscilla was gone. The Princess of the Park had returned.

CHAPTER 14

Nilan National Park

G abriel turned their little green Prius down the gravel road that lead to the ranger station at Nilan National Park. Magdalena, buckled in and be-bopping in the back seat, listened to her music on headphones. Her phone played the same mix she had played at the dance party in the park. The mix had become Magdalena's favorite. She knew why, too. Anything that started at the park made her happy. Because her time in the park made her the happiest of any time spent anywhere doing anything.

Gabriel put the car in park. The tall joyful man stepped out and walked around to the passenger side. Shewan rolled down the window. Gabriel poked his head inside, kissed her on the cheek and said, "I'm just going to go in and get the key. I paid for the cabin on-line when I booked it last spring. In just a few minutes we'll be unpacking and exploring!"

Gabriel loved the family's October camping trip. He and Shewan had been going up to Nilan National Park since they were in college together. The autumn trips were his favorites. The days were still warm enough for swimming, but the nights were cool and crisp. The sun set earlier and Magdalena might manage to stay awake for all the camp songs. Staying awake just wasn't that easy after a day playing outside and a dinner roasted over an open fire.

The United States Park Service rented out Nilan's three old ranger cabins. Gone were the resident rangers, but the cottages they used to live in were still there. They had wood stoves and electricity but no running water. Campers who rented them shared the park's public bathroom with the tent campers and day hikers.

Gabriel walked into the visitor lodge. That log cabin had been built in the 1930s by workers hired through a government plan called "The New Deal." So many people were out of work and homeless, with no way to feed themselves or their families that President Franklin Roosevelt devised a plan to hire thousands of these displaced individuals. Folks all across the country went to work improving access to the nation's natural resources.

It made Gabriel happy to know that poor people in search of a better life built the cabins at Nilan National Park. Folks who needed a paycheck and loved the outdoors worked for an agency called the Civilian Conservation Corps. Today the United States is peppered with parks and wildlife areas enhanced by their efforts.

Gabriel loved the smell of the ranger station. So many fires had been built in the old place that visitors could smell the wood fire even if none was burning at the time. This was the case when Gabriel walked into the deserted room. He looked across the entry way to the wall at the back of the cabin. By the map of Nilan National Park, next to the posters warning against forest fires and explaining proper trash disposal, hung three lock boxes. Gabriel took a slip of paper from his wallet. He'd written down the code for lock box C when he ordered their cabin that spring. The on-line website recommended writing the code down, because there was no wifi at the park and virtually no cell phone signal. He pressed the buttons numbered 5 9 5 3, and the box opened. The key for cabin C fell into his hand.

Gabriel squeezed his hand shut around the key. He frowned at the automated system for check-in and wondered how much longer the park would use keys. He remembered back to the day when a human would be at the desk to register guests. A fire – not just the smell of one

87

– would be in the fireplace. But technology had made that ranger job unnecessary. Lock boxes and on-line payment in advance eliminated those hospitality jobs entirely. Nilan National Park was once part of a program to create jobs by expanding service to communities. Now the park didn't have even one nice person with a smile to say, "Hello," to campers or reminded them that only they could *prevent forest fires.*

"No wonder there are no jobs for people without educations," Gabriel said under his breath to no one. "Glad I got an engineering degree when I did. Who knows where I'd find work if I hadn't."

Gabriel's older brother had been nothing but trouble. Gabriel, five years younger and a quick learner, kept his nose in a book while his mom struggled to keep his brother out of detention centers and eventually out of jail. She failed. Joseph, Gabriel's brother, was serving a 10 year sentence upstate at Ben Carson federal penitentiary for a spate of armed bank robberies.

Gabriel's smile faded a little remembering his brother, his broken-hearted mother and the hard work he put into school – just so he wouldn't end up like Joseph. He sighed, "I'm the luckiest man alive. I went to a good school where I met my beautiful wife, Shewan. We have a near perfect kid, Magdalena, who has her mom's brilliant brains and intense beauty. And now we make regular vacation trips to this ghost town of a national park. Yup. I'm the luckiest man alive."

Standing alone in the ranger station, Gabriel whispered one last thing to himself, "One of these days, I've got to stop talking to myself." He smiled at his words, and with the cabin key in his hand and his memories tucked back in his head, he stepped outside to begin their annual autumn adventure.

CHAPTER 15

Big Restroom - Small World

abriel unloaded the car, while Shewan unpacked each package as he unloaded them. They only had three days together for their holiday, but Shewan liked the cabin best if she could pretend she lived there all year round.

Maggie poked her head in the screen door, "Shewan, when will you be ready to walk up to the restroom with me? I really need to go."

Shewan put the last of the plates and glasses on the shelf above the cook stove and smiled at her daughter. Chuckling, Shewan replied, "You silly goose. You know I like to put everything in its place when I first arrive. You might've waited forever if you hadn't said something."

Maggie stood in the doorway with her legs crossed and whispered, "Well, it does feel like forever."

Her mom continued, "Do I have a minute to grab my shower stuff? I had a long day at work. Let me get my shampoo and soap, and I'll walk you up there while your dad builds a fire.

It'll take him a little while, so we can get a shower in at the same time."

Gabriel set the sleeping bags on the bunks and winked at his wife, "I heard that," he said. "I bought dried wood from the farmer on Oak Road last week. This fire shouldn't take too long, but you two take your time. I prefer to cook on the coals once they've burned down for a while anyway. The food doesn't burn as easy when the coals are low."

Shewan nodded and smiled. The family didn't need to rush for anything for three days. Maggie's parents enjoyed that lazy feeling as much as any of the other part of their camping trip.

Shewan thanked Gabriel for his flexibility and praised his fire building skills, "Well, you have gotten really good at campfires over the years. I was just teasing you. If Magdalena doesn't mind, I'll just grab my stuff and we can get cleaned up now instead of later."

Maggie shrugged and said, "Yeah, it's okay. I'm not that bad. I actually expected you to take a while getting ready. So I asked you before I got desperate."

Shewan good-naturedly tugged on one of her daughter's pigtails then ran into the bedroom and grabbed a towel and her overnight kit. Shewan kept all her toiletries in a plastic bucket. When they finished showering, Shewan always set her bath items back in their place and trotted back to the cabin without having to fuss with the wet bottles or bars of soap.

After they found their pajamas in their rucksacks, Shewan and Maggie joined hands and walked past Gabriel. He'd finished unpacking and had begun working at the fire pit. Half the leaves from the trees overhead were already littering the ground around the campfire area. Gabriel collected armfuls of the dry tinder and made a bed for the wood from Oak Road.

As his favorite people in the world walked by, Gabriel swung his arms high overhead. "What should I get ready for dinner?" Gabriel asked. His axe glided through the air and sank solidly into a piece of wood on the chopping block in front of him. Then seeing the bucket and towels in their arms, Maggie's dad answered his own question, "Oh never mind. I already forgot. You two are gonna be gone a while."

"Not too long. You may not have time to chop all that wood." Shewan pointed to the enormous woodpile Gabriel had pulled out of the trunk of their car. "We're just getting cleaned up now. You build the fire and get the coals ready. We'll cook together when we get back." Shewan leaned in for a kiss and then finished explaining, "I figured that if we've got our camping jammies on before supper then we can tell stories and sing campfire songs right up to bedtime."

"Good idea, Shewan!" Gabriel set down the axe, tapped his index finger at the side of his head and looked at his daughter, "I tell ya, Maggie, that mom of yours is always thinking."

Maggie smiled at her dad and turned to walk with her mom. Given all day to try, not one of Maggie's little family could have thought of a happier moment.

Nilan National Park had a great big bathroom. The porcelain fixtures had set up there in the oversized log cabin for decades, but they all worked great. Maggie and Shewan pushed the restroom door open together. The door – held in place by a twelve-pound spring – took a lot of shoving. Maggie looked at her mom and asked, "Do you think that's to keep animals out?"

"More than likely," Shewan answered. "I don't think it would give way very easily for much less than a grizzly bear and we don't have grizzly bears around here."

"We don't?" Maggie frowned. "That's too bad. I'd love to see a grizzly bear."

"Not when you're in the shower with soap in your eyes, I bet!"

Maggie giggled, "Oh yeah, not then!"

Shewan changed the subject, "Speaking of soapy hair, you want me to go first?"

Maggie nodded, "Please. I need to use the restroom and besides…" Maggie's voice drifted off as she concentrated. She pulled a rolled up comic book out of her pants pocket and exclaimed, "I came prepared!" Maggie moved over to a table and chair by the wall. "I'll just sit over here and read until it's my turn."

Setting her bucket of toiletries into the shower stall, Shewan smiled, "I love that you always have something to read with you. You and your dad: always with your nose in a book."

After Maggie used the john, she started reading. Shewan fed quarters into the coin box on the wall and the shower kicked on with high-pressure warm water. After a minute or two of letting warm water wash over her, Shewan called out to Maggie to make sure she hadn't wandered off. Although she knew her daughter wouldn't leave without asking, Shewan couldn't keep herself from making sure. "You know why they charge for these showers don't you, Maggie?"

Maggie looked up from her comic book and paused. When she'd thought of an answer she replied, "So people don't leave them running by accident."

Impressed, Shewan spoke, "Your answer is probably right. But right now I think it's because this shower is so warm and the pressure is so heavenly that people wouldn't leave unless they ran out of money!" Thirty seconds later Shewan started to sing.

Maggie loved it when her mom sang. Shewan had such a pretty voice.

Maggie started reading again when the heavy restroom door began to budge, slowly. Someone or something – not too big – was trying to come inside. Maggie said to herself, "Well, that's no grizzly bear."

Just then a pink sneaker poked in the room. Then the attached foot and leg positioned themselves for more leverage. Finally the door swung open and a young girl flew into the room.

Without looking around at the usually deserted restroom, Beth called back over her shoulder, "I'll be out in just a minute. Just wait for me by the broken rock!"

Maggie smiled at the surprise of seeing her friend. "Hey,

Beth! Where did you come from?" Maggie jumped to her feet. She tackled Beth and continued, "How cool is this! Are you here on a camping trip too?"

Beth – equally shocked by seeing another member of the posse outside their normal surroundings – quickly smiled and hugged her friend. "Hey, Maggie!" Beth responded without answering Maggie's questions – but with a question of her own, "What are you doing here?"

Maggie laughed, "I asked you first. But I can go first. My mom and dad and I come to NNP every year for our annual autumn camping trip. I've been coming here since – seriously – since before I was born."

Beth started to squirm. She glanced over at the steam rising up from the drawn curtain in the shower stall.

"Oh," Maggie blurted, thinking out loud, "Yeah, that's my mom. She's taking the first shower and then I go. We're gonna go back to our cabin and have dinner and do campfire stuff. Hey! You wanna come with? Where's Jeff? He can come too. You here with your dad? When mom gets out of the shower we can see if dad's making enough food for all of us to have a campfire supper together."

Beth looked at her friend. Then she looked at her feet.

Maggie didn't know why her friend acted so strange, "What's the matter? You okay?"

Beth's head cleared slightly.

"Umm, Jeff's probably out by the broken rock by now. He'll worry if I don't get out there pretty quick. I just need to use the restroom and get out there I think. It's sure nice to see you, Maggie."

Then Beth darted into the bathroom stall. Inside she bolted the door. She felt her face get hot. For a few moments, Beth feared that she might cry. But her need to get her business done and get outside forced all those emotions away.

A minute or so later, Beth unbolted the door and stepped out of the stall. "Hey, Maggie." She almost sounded happy, "Thanks for the nice invite, but we'll have to do that some other time. Jeff's waiting for me, and I'm sure we've got big plans for tonight already." Hearing herself lie to one of her best friends almost brought the tears back again. Beth pushed through her sadness as she pulled on the big door with the spring. "I really got to run. Great to see you. Have a fun camping trip."

With a wave, Beth disappeared outside. The big 12-pound spring did its job and closed the door tightly after her.

Confused, Maggie considered walking outside and looking for the broken rock. Something didn't seem right. Beth wasn't the friendly noble peasant she seemed to be in the park.

Maggie called to her mom, "SHEWAN, I gotta go outside for a minute."

Just as she did the water in the shower shut off.

"Oh drat," Shewan muttered. "I didn't get all the conditioner out. Hey Magdalena, grab a quarter out of my purse will you?"

Maggie didn't want to get her mom a quarter. Maggie wanted to chase after Beth. But Maggie did as she was told. When she brought the quarter to her mom, Shewan called through the curtain, "Hey Magdalena, did I hear you talking to someone?"

Now Maggie felt like she would cry. Maggie croaked out a response, "That was Beth, from school. We're not in the same class. She has Mrs. Tarrant. But we see each other all the time, in the park. Shewan poked her shining face and goopy hair around the side of the curtain to see Maggie's face as she asked, "Seriously, from the park? Does she know?"

Magdalena realized what her mom wanted to know. "Does she know Priscilla? Yeah Mom, of course she does."

Shewan stared at her daughter skeptically, "Well, what do you know about that? An eyewitness? Where'd she go?" Shewan stuck her dripping head even further out from behind the shower curtain to look around.

Magdalena looked sad as she answered, "Oh she couldn't stay, she had to run off to meet her brother, I guess."

'Hmmm," Shewan looked confused. "Well, let's finish up here and maybe we can find out who else rented a cottage this weekend. We can go back to the ranger station and see if any of the other key boxes are open. Then we'll know where your friend is staying."

Magdalena loved that idea. "Okay!" she shouted and dropped the quarter into the shower concession box. "Hurry up in there, will ya, Shewan. I need to shower before we go find Jeff and Beth."

CHAPTER 16
Safe at Home

Jillian rolled up the walkway toward the house. Her dad waved from the riding lawn mower as Jillian's chair coasted to a stop. Edgar, Jillian's favorite man on earth, switched off the mower's engine so he could talk to his daughter. "How'd it go at the Hamilton? Did you leave any onion rings for anyone else?"

Jillian smiled and pulled a grease-stained bag from the backpack on her lap, "No, I did not. But I might have been able to, if we hadn't had to get you the heaviest bag of onion rings that the Hamilton makes."

"Oh yum," Edgar growled as he leapt from the seat of the riding mower. "Gimme those now before you eat them."

Jillian rolled her eyes, then she rolled her chair toward her dad. She assured him, "Don't you worry. I'm so full I will never eat another onion ring."

"Never say never," Jillian's mom spoke up from behind as Jillian's chair got much easier to operate.

"Thanks for the added shove. I think I'm too stuffed to

push myself up the ramp," murmured Jillian. The little girl closed her eyes and let her mom drive for a while. She could hear her parents high-five as they passed each other and then she felt her chair tilt as it climbed the ramp.

Vivian and Edgar had been high-fiving since junior high. The slap of their hands meeting had gotten louder and more regular over the years. Vivian pulled down on the wheelchair's handles and popped a wheelie similar to the ones Jillian had done on her own at the park that day. When she tilted the chair back she saw Jillian's closed eyes. Vivian asked, "Pretty tired today, huh? Did you have fun?"

Jillian slowly opened one eye and answered, "We had so, so, SO much fun, dancing in the park. Beth and Jeff's dad showed up. His name is Ken. He's funny. You'd like him I think." Jillian closed her one open eye and continued talking, "Ken spoke to Priscilla a little bit. They looked pretty serious. But I think they were okay."

Vivian put Jillian's wheelchair back down on the ground. "Oh, wow, another parent has already met Priscilla. Do you think it will be safe for Priscilla? To meet this Ken guy, I mean. Remember that I'm planning to go see her myself on Tuesday. Do you think Ken will tell anyone that Priscilla might be homeless? Should we get back into the car and go over there now, ourselves?"

Jillian opened both her eyes and saw Edgar standing in front of her. His fists were on his hips as he did his best superman impersonation. Jillian pouted and looked at him. Then she craned her head back to see her mom.

Edgar spoke, "It's okay. Mom told me about Priscilla. We are in complete agreement that she needs to be protected from abuse by the parks and rec department, from the police or from anyone and everyone who might try to mess with her. But we also want to make sure she lives somewhere better than a park. We just don't know how to make that happen. Maybe we shouldn't wait until Tuesday. Maybe we should all go talk to her right now."

Jillian just frowned. A solitary tear rolled down her cheek.

"Oh, baby," Edgar moaned and dropped onto one knee before his little girl. "No, no, no, this isn't supposed to make you cry. We want to help."

Jillian kept breathing deeply – slowly in and slowly out – like her physical therapy aka yoga instructor had shown her. Jillian wasn't doing her yoga breathing to stretch out her back this time though. She was doing her yoga breathing to stretch out her mind.

Vivian had come around the chair and skootched down next to Edgar. Jillian stared at both of them, fighting the urge to start crying. Jillian suspected that if she started crying, she might find it difficult to stop.

Finally, Jillian reached forward and brushed her mom's hair out of her eyes. "How can you see with your hair in your eyes like that?" Jillian didn't just sound like the mom in the group – she looked serious enough to be the mom.

Jillian continued, "Don't take this wrong, but I don't expect you to get it. I know you're the grown-ups here and you're supposed to know this stuff better than us kids do. But what you think is helping Priscilla just isn't. I'm glad you want to meet her, but I don't want you racing over there like you know how she should live. Because you don't. Nobody does."

Vivian and Edgar, stunned into silence by their wise young daughter, sat back on their heels together. Then Edgar pulled Vivian down onto the porch beside him. They both sat legs crossed and listened.

Vivian whispered to Jillian, "Go on. What do you know about this that you need to teach us?"

"Remember I told you that Vinny saved her stuff that time the park and rec guys tried to take it?"

Her mom nodded. Edgar nodded too because Vivian had filled him in on the story after he got home from work the night Jillian had told it to her.

"Well, after they left, Vinny told me that someone got Priscilla a home once before. They came and took her away to a senior center about six miles up U.S. Route 20. Priscilla hated it. She had no way to get to the store. She had no friends. She had no community."

Edgar spoke then – trying to be gentle with his words, "Oh Jillian, she just needed to give it a better chance. Those old folks homes, they have community rooms and a van shuttle. She'd get the hang of it after a while."

Edgar realized instantly that he'd said the wrong thing. He didn't know what he said wrong, but from Jillian's reaction he knew that it was – for a fact – very wrong.

Jillian's choked back tears turned into a downpour. It took a few minutes but Jillian calmed down enough to speak. "Oh dad, see what I mean? You don't get it. YOU might get used to it. You think being homeless is terrible. So in your mind, you put yourself in that situation and convince yourself that it would be easier to get used to being alone. You think you'd rather be isolated than spend years sleeping on a bench.

"People probably think being in a wheelchair is terrible. But it's no big deal for me is because the other parts of my life are comfortable and safe. I have you and mom. I live in a space that is familiar to me. I have a cat who loves me. What if someone said they could help me walk if I left you. What if all I had to do, to be able to walk, is to leave my home? Leave you? Do you think that I'd give any of you up for the convenience of walking?"

Jillian hung her exhausted head on her heaving chest. "I'm protected here. Don't you understand? I'm happy here. Making it easier on me won't make it better. Me walking is just someone else's idea of easy."

Both her parents wrapped their arms around her and each other, forming a huddle bubble on the front porch. Edgar buried his face between Vivian and Jillian's faces and said, "I'm sorry, baby. I didn't realize how much I'd been taking for granted. Being homeless looks so awful. I never thought of it as a community. I never thought about surroundings or distances to the store being familiar or important. I'm sorry. Please don't cry."

But, of course, at that point they were all crying. Vivian picked her head up and said, "I'm glad we had this talk. When

I see Priscilla on Tuesday I'll be sure to find out what she wants and not just tell her what I think she should want."

With that the little family entered their home never so grateful to have each other as they were at that moment.

Vivian crawled into bed next to Edgar.

Edgar asked, "She asleep?"

"Are you kidding? She hit the bed sleeping." Vivian looked at her husband and asked, "You okay?"

Edgar put aside the book he held and used his arms to hold his wife instead. With one hand he tilted her face to his and said, "I'm really pretty troubled by what our daughter said about giving up her family to walk again. First of all, is that really what it's like to relocate a homeless elderly person? And if it is, then why do they keep building the elderly housing on the outskirts of town?" Edgar kissed his wife's forehead. "Another thing. I know the decision would be practically impossible for a kid to make, but as her dad, I think I'd try to talk her into leaving us - if it meant she'd be able to walk. I mean, it would be so much better for her in the long run."

Vivian shrugged her slender shoulders, "Would it, Edgar? I'm not so sure. Living a life in isolation – without the people who love you – might be far more cruel than a physical impairment. I just don't know."

Vivian took a few deep breaths, similar to the ones her daughter took earlier in the day. Once she was sure she could go on, she spoke, "One thing's for sure though. That kid of ours has a lot on her heart for such a young person. I hate that this worries her so much."

Edgar hugged Vivian tighter. "She'll be all right," he comforted her. "I read somewhere that a million kids are homeless in the United States. More than that, even. At least our little girl just has a friend that lives in the park. She doesn't have to live in one, too."

CHAPTER 17

We Gotta Get Out of Here

Beth and Jeff ran straight back to the tent sites where the Volkswagen hid under a row of cedar trees. The car looked empty. Ken had put the front seat back. He had fallen asleep about thirty seconds after the twins left for the bathroom. When Beth and Jeff yanked the car door open hollering his name, Ken jerked awake. Pretty constantly on alert no matter how tired he became, Ken's eyelids flipped open and he bent straight forward at the waist.

"What happened, what's up, you okay?" Ken blurted.

Beth and Jeff, both jabbering at the same time, got progressively louder to be heard over each other.

Ken rubbed his eyes and put his arms out to hold his children steady. "Calm down," he pleaded. "If neither of you is bleeding, then take turns talking so I can understand you. Otherwise, show me the blood."

The twins quieted and Beth spoke first, "Let me do the talking. It's my story."

Ken led the children over to the picnic table by the car.

"Okay, Beth. What's your story," he asked.

Beth spoke calmly but rapidly, as though she wanted to get the story out for two different reasons. She wanted her dad to understand the importance of what she was telling him, and she wanted him to understand it quickly so he could act on the information right away.

Beth told her dad, "I need you to listen carefully, Dad. It's vitally important that you pay close attention." Ken smiled at her use of the word, "vitally." He responded. "Fair enough, but I hope you know, I always listen carefully and pay attention to you guys. Especially when you're so wound up."

Jeff, exasperated by a conversation that he thought wasted time, blurted out, "Short of it is, Dad, one of the kids from school is camping in the park. And she saw us. Well, she saw Beth, anyway."

Beth turned to her brother and yelled, "Jeff, I was talking."

Ken hushed both of them, "Look, calm down. Don't let your concern over being discovered here let you turn on each other. Panic is not your friend."

Ken turned to look into Beth's big brown eyes, "Look Beth, lots of people come to Nilan National Park. It's a national park, for crying out loud. That's why they're here. What did your friend say when she saw you? Did she say, 'Hi, Beth, I bet you're here because you live in a car?'"

Beth shifter her weight from one foot to the other and looked at the ground. "No," she replied. "She said she thought it was cool that we were camping here too. That she and her parents were going to have a campfire. Then she invited us to join them."

Jeff looked anxiously at his dad and then back at his sister. Then Jeff shouted, "Dad, we can't hang around with those people! All Maggie has to do is see our car and she'll figure it out. Forget how fast her parents will catch on!" His voice kept getting louder. "Her parents will know we're homeless for sure!" he yelled.

Ken turned his gaze to his son, "Look pal, you gotta calm down. All we have to do is get into Martha and drive out of here. We can come back late, after everyone goes to sleep and sleep in the tent or just collect our stuff and stay out behind the Grocery*Mart tonight."

The kids ran over to the car and jumped into the back seat. Beth pleaded, "C'mon dad." Jeff added, "We've got to go."

Ken wasn't sure running away from this accidental meeting was for the best. Maybe Maggie's parents would understand. Maybe they would even help. Still, Ken knew he couldn't have a conversation about confiding in people with his children while they were in such a panicked state. Ken got behind the wheel. He put his seat into its upright position. As he fastened his seat belt he spoke over his shoulder to the twins in the back, "You kids buckled in?"

The children nodded. Ken smiled and said, "Good. Let's get out of here and find another place to talk."

Martha the Volkswagen – loaded with the Kritzell family – pulled away.

Out behind the grocery store, Ken and the kids sipped on green tea that he had made in the Hot Pot. He loved the little contraption. It worked off Martha's cigarette lighter. Ken felt pretty sure that such a device hadn't been invented so folks could live behind grocery stores. But it sure did come in handy for folks with nowhere else to go.

Beth spoke first, "This tea is good, Dad. Thanks for getting us away from there."

Jeff nodded.

Ken spoke next, "Maybe we shouldn't have run. Maybe having an ally or two would help us get through this mess we are in."

Beth and Jeff both shook their heads. Beth spoke up again, "Help us like Uncle Mike and Aunt Trudy?"

Ken looked at his kids and frowned, "Yeah, I guess that is always a risk."

Jeff chimed in this time, "Dad, it might not bother you, but I'd personally rather die than let those kids at school know we live in a car. Plenty of those kids might be nice, but plenty of kids are not nice too. Seriously, I mean it. I'd rather croak than risk any kid at school telling any other kid anything about us."

Ken's shoulders slumped. "Yeah, I guess you're right. It's pretty humiliating. But there is a bright side."

Beth, desperate for anything to brighten the mood, asked, "What Dad? What's the bright side?"

"It's almost over. After my next paycheck on Thursday, I'll have enough saved for a first and last month's rent as well as a security deposit. Then we can start looking for a home."

Beth smiled and reached out to hold her dad's hand, "Holy hippos, Dad! That is the best news you've ever told us."

Jeff added, "Hooray. I got only one favor to ask when that happens."

Ken smiled and asked, "Name it. What would you like?"

Jeff stared his dad straight in the eyes and asked for his favor, "When we get our place, can we never talk about being homeless again?"

A few days earlier Ken had wondered if his kids spent most of their time just pretending to be happy. The chance meeting they had with a friend at Nilan National Park gave him his answer.

CHAPTER 18

Which Cabin Is Theirs?

Once Magdalena and her mom had their camping pajamas on, they walked over to the Welcome Center. When Gabriel checked them in, all he had to do was plug a code into the lock box for Cabin One. The door fell open and would remain open until they put the key back in it, at the end of their visit. If Magdalena's little friend were staying in a cabin, that keybox would be open too. Magdalena and Shewan stood in the Welcome Center staring at just one opened lockbox.

"That doesn't make sense," Maggie told her mom. "Unless they are camping in the tent area. Let's look at the tent area and see which spots are taken."

Shewan began to frown.

Magdalena dragged her mom over to the Nilan National Park map. Each vacant tent site had a chip hanging from a nail. The nails stuck out of the grid, marking camping places on the map. The space markers looked like poker chips with holes drilled into them. Tent campers would come in and take the chip down when they selected their spot. There were three chips missing. Those campsites were all along the road which stretched between the restroom and the Welcome Center. Shewan and her daughter had already walked by those sites. None of them had Maggie's mystery friends camping there.

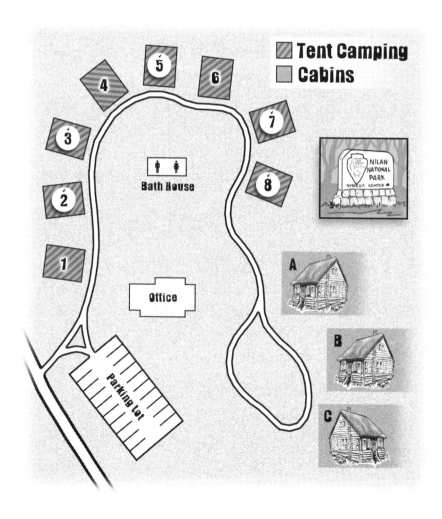

Shewan stared down at her daughter, "C'mon, let's get back to the cabin. Dad will start to worry."

Maggie kept rocking her head. She just couldn't understand why there was no sign of Beth and Jeff. Or of Ken for that matter. No sign at all.

Once they returned to the cabin, Shewan asked Magdalena to run inside and put the shower gear away. Maggie reluctantly did as she was told.

Shewan turned to Gabriel and sighed.

"What's wrong?" Maggie's dad asked Maggie's mom. "You two were happy as larks when you left for the shower."

Shewan stared up at her husband and announced, "I think we need to call the school and get a referral for Maggie to see a therapist."

"Therapist?" Gabriel nearly shouted – stunned by his wife's recommendation. "Whatever for?"

"It's this imaginary friend thing. I think it's gotten out of hand. First it was Priscilla and now Magdalena is pretending to have friends here on our camping trip."

Gabriel's head jerked backward as if he'd been hit. He asked, "Maggie thinks Priscilla is here?"

Shewan answered, "No, but she said she was talking with a friend from Priscilla's tea parties. And when we went to look for her at the Welcome Center, there was no record of this mysterious friend and her family. She had to have made the whole thing up – out of thin air."

CHAPTER 19

It Can't Be True

Tomas and Hugo walked carefully toward the park. They each held one side of Tomas's science project. Tomas took first place for the whole school. Every other kid who got an award or an honorable mention was at least two grades ahead of Tomas at Mitch Snyder Elementary and Middle School. Tomas invented a water purification system that could collect and filter sixteen ounces of rainwater at a time. The water ran off the modified lunch tray upon which Tomas had installed his filtration system and then it drained into a bottle.

Since Hugo became the protector of the realm, he's softened his attitude toward his younger brother. He hardly ever slugged him anymore, and he seldom called him a dummy or a dope. Hugo hadn't noticed the change in himself, but Tomas sure did. Of course, Tomas being smarter than the average kid meant that he was too smart to point out the change to his big brother. Rubbing Hugo's nose in his new sweetness might be a surefire way to make him resentful and angry again.

While they lugged the Royalfilter2020 toward the park, the boys barely spoke to each other. Hugo broke the silence. "You invented this for her, didn't you?"

Tomas looked back at him and smiled. "Well, yeah. This way she can have a nice cup of clean water even when they lock the bathrooms at night. And besides, when the cold weather comes and they shut the drinking fountain off in a month or so – she'll need a way to get water."

Hugo wrinkled his nose and took one hand from a corner of the Royalfilter2020 to scratch his head. "They turn the water off in the park?" he asked.

"Sure they do." Tomas sometimes felt sorry for his brother. Tomas thought about how much he took his own brainpower for granted. Or at least he used to, before he matured past Hugo's grade level. Once Tomas got into the accelerated classes, he found himself explaining many things to Hugo that seemed simple on face value. This was one of those times. Tomas told his big brother, "If they leave the water pipes that run to the outside open in the winter, they might freeze and burst. So they turn the pipes off when the weather turns cold. It's almost Halloween, so it won't be long now."

Hugo looked confused. He switched hands to scratch his head again, only this time with the one that had been holding his side of the Royalfilter2020. Hugo wasn't just nicer since he got his title from Priscilla. He also seemed less self-conscious about confessing when he didn't understand things. Something about Priscilla recognizing his protective nature made him feel better about his shortcomings. Nobody could

120

be good at everything. Hugo knew that. The only thing was, before Priscilla knighted him, Hugo hadn't realized that he was good at anything.

But Hugo was good. He was really good at protecting the little kids. And he knew it. So what if he wasn't good at figuring stuff out. That was what Tomas did well – and truth be told – it would be a disaster if they switched jobs. If Tomas was the protector of the realm, they'd have no protection at all.

Hugo stopped thinking and started talking, "Wait a minute."

Tomas stopped in his tracks – acting more out of instinct than conscious thought.

"No," Hugo corrected him. "Don't physically wait a minute. I mean – this doesn't make sense."

Tomas sometimes had to explain things more than once to Hugo so he resumed walking and asked, "Which part? The pipes freezing part? Or the pipes run outside the building part?"

Hugo shook his head from side to side, "No!" He hollered. "The it's too cold for water to be outside but it's not too cold for Priscilla to be outside part."

Tomas looked over at his brother and sighed, "Yeah. That doesn't make much sense to me either. But I guess it does to whoever gives apartments out in this town."

Hugo stopped this time, "Is that how it works? Somebody gives apartments out and they just won't give one to Priscilla? Why not? Did they run out?"

The conversation made Tomas sad. He sensed it making Hugo a little sad too. Although in Hugo's case, maybe mad was a better word. Hugo liked solving problems, not thinking about them. Tomas replied, "Look, we're almost there. I can't wait to give Priscilla her Royalfilter2020. We'll need to stop talking about this because we'll see her soon."

Then he turned to his big brother and whispered, "Hugo, all I know about the apartments is that they cost money. Mom and Dad pay for ours, but I heard Mom say we couldn't afford to live where we do if Bela hadn't come to live with us. It takes three adults to pay for our place. And Priscilla's just one adult. Where would she ever be able to live?"

That made sense to Hugo and the pair kept walking. Carrying their awkward package made them the last ones to arrive for their regular Tuesday Tea. They turned the corner and saw a huge crowd in front of Priscilla's throne. Magdalena was there. So was Jillian. She had two grown-ups with her. The twins were there too. And Vinny. He sat on Priscilla's throne. He had his mandolin in one hand. He used both arms – moving them up and down – to make a "calm down" motion.

Tomas dropped his side of the project leaving Hugo to muscle the whole thing by himself. He glanced back at Hugo to see if he was okay. Hugo said, "Yeah, I got this the rest of the way. You run along and see what's up."

Tomas got to the park bench – to the throne – and croaked out his question, "Hey, where's Priscilla?"

At first nobody answered. The little crowd looked shocked.

Then Vinny looked over at Tomas and said two words.
Two horrible terrible empty words.

Vinny said, "She's gone."

THE
Charles Bruce
F O U N D A T I O N
HELPING WRITERS ARTISTS AND MUSICIANS

The Charles Bruce Foundation works to provide creative outlets for Writers, Artists and Musicians (WAM!). Publishing Priscilla the Princess of the Park as a collaborative effort between Pat LaMarche and Bonnie Tweedy Shaw allowed the Charles Bruce Foundation to raise matching funds to support Bonnie's burgeoning career as an illustrator. Funds raised through private donation were augmented by the Pennsylvania Council on the Arts.

Consequently, Bonnie Tweedy Shaw received state arts funding support through a grant from the Pennsylvania Council on the Arts, a state agency funded by the Commonwealth of Pennsylvania and the National Endowment for the Arts, a federal agency.

All proceeds from sales of *Priscilla the Princess of the Park* benefit the needs of others. Bulk orders are available by contacting admin@charlesbrucefoundation.org.

Other publications
from the Charles Bruce Foundation

Left Out In America
Pat LaMarche

Daddy, What's the Middle Class?
Pat LaMarche

A Special Present
Pat LaMarche
Max Donnelly

My Cat is a Hat
Phyllis J. Orenyo
Chad Bruce

The Train Whistle and the Lily Pond
Arlyn Pettingell

The Secret Ingredient
Marianne Romagnoli
Nancy Stamm

The Boy with the Patch
Matthew C. Donnell
Fran Piper

If You Should Meet an Elephant
Ashley E. Kauffman
Bonnie Tweedy Shaw

Bonnie Tweedy Shaw's dad was a minister, so she moved around quite a bit. Born in Ohio, she spent her early years there, then moved to Florida before her family settled in Pennsylvania. Bonnie had eight brothers and sisters. Her big family loved camping. They'd camp for a entire month every year. They had a boys' tent, a girls' tent and their parents slept in a pop-up camper. Bonnie's oldest brother got a tiny tent all by himself! Growing up this way made Bonnie certain of one thing – life would've been very difficult if her family had lost their home and camping was their way of life.

Bonnie's love affair with art began as soon as her hand could hold a crayon. She went to Shippensburg University and received her Bachelor's Degree in art. She shifted focus for grad school, studying GeoEnvironmental Studies. In her spare time she taught undergraduates as a grad assistant to the Art Department. Today, Bonnie's still teaching. Her art classes are popular throughout central Pennsylvania. Bonnie also sculpts and paints magnificently.

When Bonnie's not creating art, home with her husband, Peter, playing with Chumley their cat or Dewey their dog, she can be found at the library. She adores working in the Youth Services department, where she talks to young patrons about their favorite books. Bonnie's first published work, *If You Should Meet an Elephant*, is available through the Charles Bruce Foundation and wherever fine books are sold.

Pat LaMarche, born in Providence, Rhode Island, graduated Boston College and went to grad school at the University of Amsterdam. Pat has two kids and a step kid – Rebecca, John and Eden. She adores them (and their partners – Tim and Kaede). Pat's also got a couple of spectacular grandchildren, Ronan and Maggie. Though Pat lived most of her adult life in Maine, she now resides with her husband, Chad, in Carlisle, Pennsylvania. For more than a decade, Pat has worked sheltering and advocating for people experiencing homelessness.

Pat crisscrossed the United States, nearly a dozen times, interviewing the nation's most economically challenged families and individuals. She's witnessed hundreds of different programs to mitigate their suffering. Too many of those attempts never addressed the fundamental cause of homelessness, resulting in failure. Pat's documented their stories in countless news articles and commentary.

Having written about homelessness, poverty and health care since the last century, her other titles include, *Left Out In America: the State of Homelessness in the United States*, *Daddy, What's the Middle Class?*, *Magic Diary*, and *The Special Present*. *Left Out in America – Again*, a fifteen year anniversary edition of her original book on homelessness is due out in the fall of 2020.

More Praise for *Priscilla the Princess of the Park*

If adults are truly interested in learning about homelessness, this children's book will do it. The characters are as real as the storyline. Pat LaMarche nailed it!

Diane Nilan, President and Founder, Hear Us, National advocate for families and youth experiencing homelessness

Priscilla the Princess of the Park draws readers into the highs and lows of being homeless. One can't help but become invested in the lives of Priscilla and her young friends. Buckle up, because you're in for a ride filled with laughter, acceptance, concern and love.

Sonia Pitzi, LIU 12 Region 3 Coordinator Education for Children and Youth Experiencing Homelessness (ECYEH)

Priscilla the Princess of the Park gives names, faces, and stories to the millions of men, women, and children facing homelessness in America on a daily basis. She lovingly reveals their true identities; our classmates, friends, coworkers, and the occasional princess in the park.

Heather Denny, State Coordinator for Homeless Education, Montana Office of Public Instruction